Dangerous Moonlight

***Other Five Star Titles
by Tess Pendergrass:***

Colorado Shadows

Dangerous Moonlight

Tess Pendergrass

Five Star • Waterville, Maine

This novel is a work of fiction. Names, characters, places and incidents are either the product of the author's imagination, or, if real, used fictitiously.

Five Star First Edition Women's Fiction Series.

Published in 2002 in conjunction with
Martha Longshore.

Set in 11 pt. Plantin by Myrna S. Raven.

Printed in the United States on permanent paper.

Library of Congress Cataloging-in-Publication Data

Pendergrass, Tess.
  Dangerous Moonlight / Tess Pendergrass—Five Star 1st ed.
    p. cm.
  ISBN 0-7862-3705-8 (hc : alk. paper)
  I. Title.
PS3566.E457 D47 2002
  813'.6—dc21   2001051238

Dangerous Moonlight

Chapter 1

"Please can you help me? Please? I've just been murdered."

Detective Daniel Parks missed a step, sloshing coffee over his hand. Fortunately, the coffee maker had turned itself off an hour before. He wiped the lukewarm liquid onto his pants and turned toward the front desk.

"I mean, I'm not dead, but I might have—I mean, someone just tried to kill me."

The woman clutching the front counter, stammering her story to Nancy Dennis, the department receptionist, did not look like a crank. Except for her mahogany-colored hair, which frizzed around her head like the mane of a Shih Tzu having a bad-hair day, she reminded Daniel of a young Audrey Hepburn—finely sculpted features, porcelain-smooth skin, and dark, earnest eyes that hinted at mischief. She was beautiful.

Daniel grimaced. He'd have preferred a crank. Twenty more minutes of paperwork and he'd be through with this long, miserable day, sitting at home watching the Oakland–Chicago game while he reheated last night's spaghetti. He already knew the As had won, four to two. Everyone in the department knew he taped the As games, and they delighted in spoiling the suspense for him. But he watched the games anyway. The complex geometry of baseball untangled his mind from the stress of his job.

This day had been even more stressful than most. Before he'd finished his first cup of coffee, he'd been called to a domestic dispute that had escalated to attempted homicide, with the wife-beater being transported to the hospital with a head fracture and the wife-beater's brother-in-law arrested and on his way to jail. The day had sprinted downhill from there.

Then, not half an hour before his shift was over at five, the call on County Supervisor Gage Barclay's plane had come in. If the plane had crashed another twenty feet across Prairie Hill Road, it would have been the Jasper County sheriff's headache. But it must have been the sheriff's lucky day. It certainly hadn't been Daniel's. He'd supervised the scene before driving out to inform Mrs. Barclay of her husband's death. That hadn't been easy, either. He'd attended high school with Fiona Brooks Barclay.

Now this. Twenty more minutes and this beautiful woman and her assault report would have been Sergeant Dillon's problem. Technically, she already was—Ben Dillon was the investigator on call tonight. Daniel's shift had ended—he checked his watch—almost four hours ago. Nancy could call Ben. If Daniel remembered right, the man was at his oldest daughter's piano recital.

Daniel cursed beneath his breath. He knew how tough being an investigator could be on family life, on a marriage. Knew it firsthand.

"Detective Parks?" Nancy gestured him over. "I think you'd better hear this."

Ben owed him one.

"Detective Daniel Parks," he introduced himself, stepping to the front desk. The woman across the counter looked at him, the skepticism in her eyes reminding him even more forcefully of Audrey Hepburn. Belatedly, he remembered he'd left his tie sitting on his desk, and his rolled-up shirtsleeves were streaked with grease from the plane crash investigation.

He was glad the desk hid her view of his grass- and coffee-stained pants.

8

"Des—Destiny Millbrook," the woman replied, her voice shaking as she tried to catch her breath.

She'd either been running or badly frightened. Or both. Daniel noticed that her attire—jeans and a mulberry-colored T-shirt under a denim jacket—looked as disheveled as his own. Though that didn't diminish the overall effect of the casual way the clothes hugged her curves.

"Did I hear you say that you were assaulted, Ms. Millbrook?"

"Yes." Stress pinched the word to a squeak. "Oh, God. Someone tried . . ." She swallowed.

No blood. He saw no obvious bruises, though the flourescent lighting in the station lobby yellowed most Caucasian skin tones to a uniform level of jaundice. Her pupils looked normal. But she was still panting heavily.

No. Not her. He leaned warily over the counter and looked down into the wide brown eyes of a large, cream-colored Labrador retriever. The dog was sitting obediently at her mistress's side, but her flattened ears and shallow respiration revealed intense stress.

"It's all right, Ms. Millbrook." Daniel used his most reassuringly official tone, trying to calm both the woman and the dog. "You're safe here. Are you injured? Should we call an ambulance for you?"

She shook her head, her wild hair dancing. Was that a red mark on her neck? Daniel got a bad feeling in the pit of his stomach. If that was a recent hickey, this was going be a lot more complicated than a mugging on the Square on a Friday night.

Husband? She didn't wear a ring. Boyfriend. Lover's quarrel. Whatever it was, the stark, battered lobby was not the place for a victim to have to tell her story, despite how quiet the police department was for a weekend evening. The flickering lighting and tomblike closeness of the basement of City Hall might give a suspect something to think about, but Daniel would be happy to give up that small advantage of intimidation when the city council finally made good their promise of renovation.

"Ms. Millbrook, why don't you come into my office? I'll get you a cup of coffee, and you can tell me what happened." *No, not the coffee, Parks,* he reminded himself. The department coffee was never good, but tonight it could qualify as police brutality.

"No." The word was a burst of frustration. "You don't understand. I need to take you . . . It's not just that he attacked me. I . . . ." Her voice wavered.

Nancy interrupted by patting the woman's hand, which still grasped the edge of the front counter. "You need to sit down, ma'am. Detective Parks will help you. I'm sure he'll let you take your dog into the office with you."

Daniel shot the receptionist a look. "Ms. Millbrook, just follow me—"

"I fought back!" Destiny Millbrook burst out. Daniel saw that she was shaking. "I knocked him out. I—I might have killed him."

Daniel stared at her for only a second. "Nancy—"

"I'm on it." Nancy already had the dispatch microphone in hand, calling the paramedics.

Daniel turned to his not-so-helpless victim. "Where should I send them?"

"The park," she said. "From the parking lot, it's the main path to the gazebo."

"Nancy, I'll need a crime-scene unit."

"I'll round one up."

"Thanks. Who's available to come with me?"

"I can lead you there," Destiny offered. He could see fear

in her eyes. Not just fear of what had happened to her, but also fear of him. Fearing the police was a healthy response from anyone who might have committed a homicide, justified or otherwise. But it still bothered him. The vulnerability in those dark eyes moved him—a reaction he had experience enough to squelch.

"The faster we can find him, the better," he agreed. "But I need another officer to accompany us, since we know the man is dangerous."

"Kermit's in back, about to go off duty," Nancy said.

"Riggs!" Daniel bellowed, checking the gun in his shoulder holster and patting his shirt pocket to make sure he had his notebook.

Kermit Riggs stuck his head out the doorway of the officers' lounge as Daniel pushed through the swinging half door at the end of the counter.

"You're with me," Daniel barked, pretending not to notice the way the young officer's eyes lit up at the opportunity to see action.

Despite Kermit's gangly, youthful appearance and reputation as a klutz, Daniel believed he had the makings of a first-rate officer. Twelve years on the Hope Point police force had taught Daniel to trust his instincts.

Unfortunately, Kermit's instincts weren't yet as finely tuned as his own. One glance at Destiny Millbrook had the young man running a hand through his painfully short blond hair and straightening the front of his uniform.

"Possible homicide," Daniel told him. The distraction caused Kermit to trip over the lip of the doorway as they followed Destiny and her dog out into the parking lot. The air, cool but not yet cold, felt good on Daniel's arms.

"It's probably faster if we walk," he suggested. The park's west entrance was only half a block from the police station.

"Fleur and I ran over here," Destiny agreed, hurrying toward the street. The big Lab pressed tight against her thigh, making her stride awkward, but it still took Daniel a minute to pull abreast of her.

"How far into the park?" he asked.

"From this direction, past the gazebo and then to the creek. Maybe a third of a mile." Tension radiated from her.

Daniel kept his pace just below a trot. He, too, wanted to hurry, but Destiny was still having trouble catching her breath. Also, he needed to know what he and Kermit would be facing when they arrived.

"Lovers' quarrel?"

"What?" Destiny missed a step, snapping her head around to stare at him.

"Is that what the fight was about?" Daniel pushed.

"No! I didn't even know the man."

"Then what were you doing in the park with him?"

Even in the dim light from the street lamp at the end of the block, he could see the color rise in her cheeks. Amber fire drove some of the fear from her eyes.

"I wasn't 'in the park with him,' " she said, between heavy breaths. "I was in the park by myself . . . minding my own business . . . when he attacked me."

"I see." Daniel kept his voice noncommittal. Since she had admitted to violence of her own, he could no longer take her words at face value without further confirmation.

"We turn here," Destiny said, pointing to a crushed-stone path that led from the sidewalk through the manicured lawn at the entrance of the park. They turned, moonlight soon overpowering the lamplight behind them, silvering the white rocks that crunched beneath their feet. The dusky glimmer led them toward the dark trees, the redwoods' high crests outlined by stars.

12

Sequoia Pacific Park, named for the local lumber company that had donated the playground equipment and the lodge, consisted of a well-maintained recreation area, including the playground, soccer field, and baseball diamond, and a system of developed trails in a small acreage of woods. But the park proper melded into the huge expanse of the Hope Point Community Forest, a tract of second-growth redwood forest that draped around the western edge of town and stretched all the way to the top of Redwood Hill.

Looking up at the swath of darkness flowing up the incline ahead of them, Daniel felt a surge of some primitive instinct that didn't want to take Destiny Millbrook back into that feral gloom.

"You were in the park," he said. "Where?"

"I was in the park . . . minding my own business," she repeated, gulping air to catch her breath. "I was walking from the soccer field toward the gazebo—"

"By yourself?" Kermit asked from behind them.

"I had Fleur with me," Destiny said, gesturing to the Lab. The dog's tail wagged briefly, and she whined.

"Reassuring," Daniel commented.

Destiny's glare showed spirit. "She's not usually like this. She got very upset after I was attacked. She'd run on ahead and didn't even know I was in trouble. When she came back and found me hysterical, she sort of freaked out."

She rubbed the dog's ears. "I got a big dog to make people think twice, not to attack them."

Seeing that her panic and breathing had both eased, Daniel picked up the pace. "You were on the path toward the gazebo."

"The path from the parking lot," she clarified. "I heard voices. It sounded like they were coming from the gazebo."

"It was already dark?" Daniel asked.

13

"Officially, the park's closed after dusk," Kermit said.

"Yes, it was after sunset. And I let Fleur off her leash, too," Destiny snapped, turning on Daniel. "Do you want to fine me before or after we find this guy?"

They'd entered the woods now, and the moonlight filtering through the redwood crowns barely illuminated their path. The thick carpet of redwood duff muffled all sounds except for the crunch of their shoes on the gravel.

Kermit pulled a heavy flashlight from his belt. The circle of light only emphasized the surrounding night by comparison. Daniel felt a deep urge to take Destiny Millbrook by the shoulders and shake her for wandering in here alone after sundown.

The impulse made his voice gruff. "So, it was dark. You heard voices."

"I didn't want to disturb whoever it was—"

"Probably teenagers," Kermit offered.

"They weren't making out, if that's what you're thinking," she said. "It was two men, and their voices sounded tense. I was going to turn off onto the side path that runs along the creek, to bypass them altogether. But Fleur must have smelled something interesting, because she headed straight for the gazebo."

"One of the reasons for the leash law—" Both Destiny and Daniel turned to glare at Kermit, and he snapped his mouth shut, stumbling once more, the flashlight bobbing wildly for an instant.

"Fleur's a well-trained dog," Destiny said, once again defensive. "She'd have come if I'd raised my voice, but I didn't want to disturb those men in the gazebo."

Daniel thought that was the first sensible thing she'd said that evening. Even in a small, quiet town like Hope Point, people occasionally got mugged. Generally a lost wallet was the worst consequence. But a young woman from the university had been raped and murdered in the community forest just the year before, and the nationwide plague of drugs and gangs had begun to infect even this isolated resort town on the northern California coast. Even as a police officer with a gun on his hip, he'd be wary of approaching two unidentified men in the park at night.

"There's the gazebo," Kermit said. An old-fashioned lamppost designed to discourage illegal campers spilled soft light across the clearing up ahead. It picked out the white latticework of the octagonal gazebo in the center of the open lawn.

"Fleur was crashing around in the azalea bushes there." Destiny pointed. "Somebody yelled, 'What the hell is that?' I called out that it was only my dog, sorry to disturb them, and grabbed her collar and dragged her away."

"And one of them attacked you?" Daniel kept a hand on his gun as Kermit trotted over to shine his flashlight into the gazebo. He looked back at Daniel and shook his head.

"I don't know," Destiny said, her voice unsteady once more. "I didn't hear anybody come after me, and I was listening, sort of nervous about it. I felt like an idiot, jumping at my own shadow, but something about it spooked me."

"I'm a firm believer in instinct," Daniel said. "I understand this is difficult for you. If you don't feel you can accompany us the rest of the way—"

If he was afraid she might become hysterical, the dark look she shot at him was reassuring.

"I walked this way, back the direction I'd come." She turned to the right, onto a path leading into more thick woods. "The parking lot beside the soccer field is about a quarter mile this way. Not far ahead there's a bridge crossing the creek. I'd just passed the bridge when someone grabbed me from behind."

In the bobbing of Kermit's flashlight, Daniel saw her shudder.

"He grabbed your arm?"

Another shudder. "My neck. If he'd been taller, he might have hooked me with the crook of his elbow, and I probably wouldn't have gotten away. But he grabbed me with his hands, and . . ."

Her voice trailed away, leaving Daniel to imagine the attacker's fingers digging into the soft flesh of her neck. Perhaps that was the explanation for the red marks he'd seen. His visceral response was a desire to kill the guy, but his training pushed his emotional reaction aside.

If she was telling the truth, the law would take appropriate action. And that was still a definite *if*, his sympathy for the victim notwithstanding.

"He bent me back. I couldn't run, couldn't scream. It was like one of those nightmares. I knew if I didn't do something, I'd never wake up."

She shook her head, perhaps trying to shake away the memory.

"Fleur had run ahead, and I couldn't breathe to call her. She didn't even know I was in trouble until it was over."

The faint call of sirens echoed through the trees ahead of them. The ambulance must have reached the parking lot. The paramedics should meet them somewhere along this path.

Daniel heard the gurgle of the creek before Kermit's flashlight found the picturesque footbridge that crossed it. In winter he might have paused to look for footprints, but the dry summer and the gravel path would make such an effort futile tonight.

"There, you can see the clearing." Destiny pointed toward a break in the darkness. Daniel touched her arm, indicating she should stay behind him as he gestured for Kermit to kill the flashlight. No sense in making themselves a target.

He drew his gun, hearing Destiny's gasp as the moonlight caught on the barrel. He and Kermit moved forward, the tall, awkward young officer beside him suddenly cautious as a prowling cat.

Each using a redwood tree for cover, they looked into the small grassy clearing before them. Moonlight silvered a swath of grass, and stars shone like ice chips overhead.

"See anything, Riggs?"

"No, sir."

"All right. Use the flashlight. But stay behind that tree."

The bright yellow light flared on the grass, brushing across the length and breadth of the clearing.

"Oh, my God." Destiny's voice sounded from behind Daniel's shoulder. "He's gone."

Destiny leaned against the ragged bark of a redwood tree, one hand on Fleur's warm head, as she watched Detective Parks direct his forensics team.

After searching the bushes and ranging up and down the path on either side of the clearing, the ambulance crew had returned to their vehicle empty-handed, replaced by a police photographer and a tall, skinny officer with a fingerprint kit and evidence bags. Since there was no evidence and nothing to fingerprint, Detective Parks had his people moving across the clearing in a ragged line, searching the grass for clues.

"This is hopeless," the photographer complained, even as her flashbulb flared in the dark. "The ground's too hard to show footprints, and so many people pass by here every day, I don't see how we're going to deduce anything from all the trampled grass. There could have been a struggle here—" She pointed to where a clump of grass had come up by its roots. "—but I wouldn't swear to it."

17

"Just keep looking," the detective directed as he pushed himself up from his crouch in the center of the line. He gestured for Officer Riggs to fill his place and moved back toward Destiny, the moonlight picking out his off-white shirt against his sun-darkened skin.

"While they complete their search, maybe you could finish telling me your story," he suggested in his deep, measured voice.

Irritation rippled through her. She'd led them to a crime scene, and he had his people crawling on their knees through the grass. A muffled curse filled the clearing as Officer Riggs tripped and fell on his hands.

She hadn't exactly ended up with Sherlock Holmes and Watson here. Visualizing the mental comparison, she realized she had reached the edge of her endurance. The image of Detective Parks in a Sherlock Holmes-style deerstalker hat and drooping pipe pushed her to the brink of hysterical laughter. With his rolled-up shirtsleeves and finger-combed sandy hair, the detective would look more at home in a four-wheel-drive truck than a four-horse carriage.

Yet there was an intensity to his gaze that wouldn't let her dismiss him as a bumbling incompetent.

"Do you think this is the best use of your manpower?" she asked, straightening. "The man who attacked me is running around loose somewhere."

Fleur pressed closer, hearing the quaver in her voice. The dog didn't like being back at the scene of the crime any more than she did.

"I was expecting an injured man, possibly a corpse." The detective echoed her frustration. "If I'm going to hunt down a non-corpse, I'd prefer to know what I'm looking for."

She couldn't argue with that, though his attitude challenged her to. Instead, she clenched her jaw to keep her teeth from chattering, though the sea-kissed air was not yet cold—unusual in this coastal climate, even in summertime. Adrenaline had brought her this far, but her adrenaline rush was giving way to delayed terror, despite the presence of armed police officers.

"You said the man grabbed you from behind. You fought back. How did you get away?"

He stepped in close, too close, so she had to tilt her head to meet his gaze. If he meant to intimidate her, he'd chosen the wrong victim.

"He was choking me. I was afraid I was about to black out," she said, her voice steady despite the way her throat tightened at the memory. She'd never forget an instant of that brief struggle, the man's smell of fear and sweat and aftershave. "I jabbed him in the stomach with my elbow. He let go of me for an instant, and I whacked him. He fell, and . . . and then he didn't move. I was afraid I'd killed him."

"You hit him?" The detective said slowly, "And thought you'd killed him? Are you a black belt or something?"

Fortunately for Daniel, she was not. She kept her fists clenched against her ribs. "I hit him," she said, drawing out her words in turn, "with my baseball bat. I didn't think I'd hit him *that* hard, but—" Her voice broke. "I should have checked for a pulse, but I was so scared. If he was just faking . . ."

Daniel took a half step back, releasing a long, frustrated breath. "Please, try to remember to tell me everything, even if it doesn't seem important to you. The fact that you were carrying a baseball bat, for instance. Why did you have a bat with you?"

The suspicion in his tone pulled her together. "I was hitting tennis balls for Fleur in the soccer field earlier. I just carried it with me."

19

"Did you leave it here?"

Destiny looked down at her hand, surprised to see she was not carrying the familiar ash bat in her hand.

"I don't know," she confessed. "I didn't mean to let it go. But Fleur came back, and I put on her leash, and I . . . I just don't know what happened to the bat."

"If she'd hit him very hard, we'd have found blood," the skinny officer spoke up.

The makeshift forensics team had given up the search of the clearing and now moved in behind Daniel.

"You know how head wounds bleed," he continued. "We couldn't have missed it."

"He was wearing a sweatshirt," Destiny explained. "The kind with a hood. I saw that after he fell. He had the hood pulled up, I guess to hide his face. If there was blood, maybe that kept it from reaching the grass."

Talking about it, she could hear again the sickening thud of her bat hitting his head, see the prone body, dark against the moonlit grass. She could very well have killed a man. The relief that he hadn't died mixed with the fear that he was still on the loose. For a moment a strange buzzing sounded in her ears, creating a distancing sensation that left her unsure where her feet had gone.

"Yeah, maybe." The officer didn't bother to hide his skepticism. "Is there anything more you want us to do here, Detective?"

The photographer was tucking her camera into its case. "Yeah. If you find any evidence of an actual crime, Daniel, give me a call. I'll be at home."

The skinny officer muttered something else. Destiny thought she caught the words *acid trip*. The implication that she was on drugs would have infuriated her, except the man's voice came from too far away to have any effect on her.

"I'll be sure to send you a copy of this roll of pictures, Daniel," the photographer offered. She grinned. "They ought to be spectacular. Maybe I'll set them up as an exhibit. Something like 'Portrait of the Dark Grass as a Dead Man'."

That struck Destiny as vaguely funny, but she couldn't laugh because she was desperately focused on not throwing up. The earth beneath her feet wouldn't stop shifting.

"Ms. Millbrook, are you all right?"

Daniel's hand on her shoulder kept her from spinning into the ground. She managed to shake her head. "I'm sorry," she heard herself say. "I believe I am going to pass out."

And then she did.

Chapter 2

Voices called to her, trying to wake her up. Destiny didn't know why, but she had the distinct impression she'd rather not.

"Ms. Millbrook? Destiny? Can you hear me?"

"Lay her down here."

"In the wet grass?"

"Wait, I think she's coming around."

"Ms. Millbrook?"

Destiny shook her head, burrowing deeper into the darkness. A warm darkness that smelled of soap and skin and . . . axle grease?

Sensations returned slowly to her body. She could feel the ground beneath her feet and strong arms around her waist. Fleur's wet nose pressed into her hand.

"Destiny?" Detective Parks's low voice, close by, tickled her earlobe. "You fainted."

"I gathered as much." She wanted to atone for her temporary weakness by showing him she could stand on her own, but she didn't quite trust her legs yet. "I'm sorry. I've never done that before."

Her cheek fit comfortably against his shoulder, and she decided to leave it there for the moment.

"It's my fault." His voice was gruff, but he kept his hold on her. "I should have realized you might suffer from shock. Sylvia, can I have your jacket?"

"Here." The photographer adjusted her loose khaki jacket over Destiny's own denim one. Hesitantly, Destiny tested her legs. They held, and Daniel released her. The cool air seeped around her once more.

"You ought to get her to the hospital," the skinny officer advised. "If she's OD'd—"

Daniel shook his head. "She's not on drugs."

"Come on, Detective, it's a possibility."

"No, it's not. I haven't been that lucky today."

Destiny didn't know whether to thank him or hit him.

He ran a hand through his hair. "Look, there's nothing more we can do tonight. You two go home. I'll call you tomorrow if I need you. Kermit, get a squad car and bring it to the parking lot. We'll give Ms. Millbrook a ride home."

After scattered good-byes, the clearing emptied, leaving Destiny alone with the detective.

"Can you walk to the parking lot?"

She nodded. "I think so. I'll be fine as long as I don't dwell on . . . it."

"Good. But if you feel dizzy again, let me know."

Only if banging my head against a tree doesn't work. She'd made enough of a fool of herself for one night, and it wasn't even over yet.

"It's darker now that the moon's behind the trees," she observed. Even though the other officers had just preceded them down the path, the knowledge that her attacker had survived caused the night to pulse with threat.

"Don't worry about that." A circle of light picked out the path ahead of them. "Officer Riggs left me his flashlight."

An image of the gangly young officer tripping over a tree root and breaking his neck flashed through Destiny's mind. "Will he be all right?"

Daniel's gaze snapped around to meet hers. He laughed, genuine laughter that softened the taut lines of his face and made him look younger than she'd first thought. She laughed, too, the release a blessing after the horror of the evening.

"Tim and Sylvia both have lights," Daniel assured her, his amusement settling into a wry grin. "I'm sure he'll be fine."

He led the way along the path, Destiny following close on his heels, clutching Fleur's leash. She doubted that her attacker was still waiting around for the chance to finish strangling her if she fell behind, but she'd been wrong before.

"Kermit Riggs is a very competent officer," Daniel said, holding a branch out of her way. "Despite his . . ."

"Eagerness?" Destiny supplied.

"Exactly."

Shoes crunching in the gravel, they descended a steep hill that ended where the soccer field met the parking lot, on the opposite side of the park from the police station. Streetlights lit the small, tree-enclosed lot, and Daniel clicked off the flashlight as they stepped onto the concrete.

"That's my car." Destiny pointed to the lone VW Rabbit crouching in a bright circle of lamplight. Fleur gave a tug of her leash in that direction. Destiny agreed with the dog wholeheartedly. She wanted to be home, away from the park, away from fear, away from irritable policemen. Visions of chamomile tea and a warm afghan wavered before her eyes.

"Kermit will have the squad car here in just a minute," the irritable policeman said.

"Don't worry about it," Destiny said, digging in her jean pockets for her keys. "I can drive myself home."

"I don't think your driving right now is a good idea. I'm going to take you to the hospital before I escort you home."

It took a second for the words to register. "Hospital?" she repeated, unable to keep the disappointment from her voice. "Did you decide I'm on drugs after all? Or do you think I'm an escaped mental patient? Somebody attacked me out there, Detective Parks. I didn't imagine it, and I didn't hallucinate it. And if you don't want to believe me—"

"I believe that someone attacked you." His calm voice silenced her. "And you're not exhibiting any signs of drug use. I said I believe in instinct, and mine tells me you're not delusional, but it doesn't take instinct to see that you ought to be examined."

She tensed as he raised his right hand toward her, but he brushed the curls back from her cheek with careful gentleness, exposing her neck.

"Drugs didn't put these bruises on your throat, Ms. Millbrook. And unless you're some kind of masochistic contortionist, you didn't put them there yourself. I barely noticed them at the station, which means they must have darkened since then. You should have a doctor take a look."

As his fingertips brushed over the bruises, she felt each individual imprint, remembered the bite of her attacker's fingernails, the closing of her windpipe. The pain must have been lurking behind her adrenaline-induced energy, and she grimaced at its sudden intensity. It hurt to swallow.

"But my car . . . And I can't leave Fleur here."

Flashing blue and red lights strobed the trees, announcing the arrival of Officer Riggs in the patrol car.

Daniel sighed, and Destiny understood that this hadn't been his day.

"The dog can come with us. You can pick up your car in the morning."

"I'll be towed."

"No, you won't. I've got connections."

Maybe she *was* hallucinating, because she thought he actually winked at her before moving to the driver's window of the patrol car to confer with Riggs. Her knees weakened again, but this time from relief. Police detectives did not wink at lunatics—or drug addicts. She hadn't realized how desperately she'd needed to know that someone believed her story.

She led Fleur toward Daniel, who had opened the back door of the patrol car for them. For the first time since the attack, Fleur pulled away from Destiny, eager to investigate the strange vehicle. Her tail slapped merrily against the squad car as she turned her attention to its interior, apparently a doggy paradise of smells.

"Hop in." Destiny nudged her from behind, and Fleur needed no further encouragement.

"She's a real nice dog," Officer Riggs commented with genuine enthusiasm. "Lab?"

Destiny nodded as she tugged her seat belt across her lap.

"I've never seen one that pale. Almost cream colored. Is he a show dog?"

"She's a humane society dog." Destiny grunted as Fleur's back foot landed on her thigh. She pushed, and the dog sat squarely on her lap. "Fleur!"

"I want a dog," Officer Riggs said, making cow-eyes at Fleur through the partition between the back and front seats. "Soon as I can find a place that allows pets. I was thinking a Lab or maybe a retriever."

Destiny forbore to mention that Labradors were retrievers. She managed to push Fleur's rear end off her lap and onto the seat. Fleur didn't appear to notice; she was too busy grinning at Officer Riggs. Obviously she had found a soul mate.

The slamming of the front door diverted Riggs's attention.

"The hospital?" Daniel suggested, only the faintest hint of irritation in his tone.

When Destiny realized that Daniel didn't plan to take Officer Riggs's place behind the wheel, she tightened her seat belt and placed a protective arm across Fleur. But Riggs drove with quiet competence, no trace of his clumsiness in evidence until they reached the hospital parking lot. As he tried to take off his seat belt, the shoulder strap trapped him in a headlock.

"You stay here with the dog," Daniel suggested, ignoring the officer's embarrassed struggles. "If it looks like this will take awhile, I'll come out and let you know."

Destiny would have preferred to wait until Officer Riggs had freed himself, but after instructing Fleur to be good, she followed Daniel inside.

This small-town emergency room didn't match the images she'd seen on TV. Quiet reigned in the almost claustrophobic entrance area. A nurse chatted with an older woman wearing a volunteer's nametag behind the long desk. Only an occasional noise from behind the green-sheeted cubicles off to the left indicated more activity.

The nurse, a natural blonde with deep lines edging her mouth, glanced their way. "Detective Parks. What can I do for you?"

"Hi, Jen. I've got a victim of an attempted strangulation here. She's got some ugly bruises, and she fainted about twenty minutes ago."

The nurse clucked with professional sympathy as she came around from behind the counter.

"Follow me, hon," she said to Destiny. "I'll check your blood pressure and pulse, and then we'll have Dr. Johanssen take a look at you. You have your insurance card?"

Destiny nodded.

"I'll bring you the forms while you're waiting for the doctor."

"Quiet night?" Daniel asked, following them into one of the cubicles.

The nurse settled Destiny on a folding chair. "Knock on wood."

"No head traumas? Concussions?"

27

Destiny shuddered as she realized why he'd asked the question.

The nurse shook her head. "Had a kid who broke his arm trying to jump his skateboard over the family dog. The dog woke up at a bad moment. And an older gentleman who nearly cut off his finger chopping tomatoes with a bread knife. Not much action for a full moon."

She noticed Destiny's expression. "It's a fact, hon. A full moon brings out the crazies—isn't that right, Detective?"

Daniel shrugged. "We do seem to fill out more incident reports at certain times of the month. People act strangely—like walking alone in the park after sunset."

Destiny felt the color creeping up her neck. At least he didn't know the reason she'd been in the park tonight. Speaking of full moons.

"You never did say why you were out so late," he continued, as though reading her thoughts.

"I didn't have a chance to walk Fleur earlier, and it wasn't that dark when I started out." She knew her excuse sounded lame, but she had no intention of explaining her sister's lunar theories to this detective. She would rather have him think she was on drugs.

"You weren't planning to meet someone?"

"No." That at least was the truth, though she wasn't sure he believed her.

The doctor's arrival rescued her from further questioning.

The examination didn't take long. The doctor gave her an over-the-counter analgesic for the pain, told her to go home and drink some herbal tea, and said she shouldn't have any lingering effects from her injuries.

Daniel asked the physician some questions about the positioning of her attacker's hands and his probable height. Dr. Johanssen's answers dovetailed with the flashes Destiny remembered: medium height, maybe five-eight or -nine, with short, stubby fingers.

"But you didn't get a look at his face?" Daniel asked her.

"I'm sorry." She wished now that she'd pulled back the man's hood after she decked him, but she'd been too terrified. No one in her entire life had ever tried to injure her before.

The whole evening had begun to blur around her by the time they left the hospital and she belted herself once more into the back seat of the patrol car with Fleur. The Lab panted at her with great glee, and Officer Riggs had a guilty flush to his cheeks, but Destiny chose not to mention the Twinkie crumbs stuck to Fleur's nose.

She hadn't left her porch light on. The shadows lurking around her front walk seemed thicker and darker than usual as she climbed out of the patrol car. No lights shone in the houses up and down her quiet street. Except for the downtown bars, Hope Point pretty much rolled back its sidewalks after eleven, even on a Friday night.

Fleur didn't notice her nervousness. She bounded past Destiny, thumping an impatient foot against the front door, leaving a fresh set of scratches in the white paint.

"I am reminded of why some landlords don't allow dogs," Daniel commented, joining her on the sidewalk.

"I'll repaint the door before I move out," she answered sourly. Detective Parks was probably a cat person. Still, she was glad to have him walk her to her door, his solidity beside her comforting as she fumbled with her key. Strange how the flare of lights dispelled less darkness than did the presence of another human being.

He stayed on the stoop as she stepped through the doorway, Fleur dashing toward the kitchen and the cookie jar.

29

"Des—, I mean Ms. Millbrook—"

"Destiny is fine. Even the sixth-graders don't call me Ms. Millbrook."

"Sixth graders?"

She noticed that his eyebrows crinkled together when he couldn't follow a conversation. It was disconcertingly appealing.

"Seventh-graders soon. I coach a summer softball league."

"Ah. The baseball bat."

"The baseball bat."

"You said you took it to the park to hit tennis balls?"

She nodded, feeling the odd guilt of being doubted even though she told the truth. "Fleur can chase tennis balls for hours. The bat saves my arm."

"Why didn't you take it back to the car before your walk?"

She shrugged, uncomfortable. "It would have taken more time, and I wanted to get our walk over before it got too late." Then, the truth. "I felt better with it, in the twilight."

"Huh." He paused. "Have you thought about carrying pepper spray?"

They were standing in her open doorway, letting in mosquitos and cold air, and he was asking her about pepper spray.

"I've thought about it, but as I said, I don't usually walk after dark. During the day, Fleur and I couldn't avoid all the joggers and mountain bikers in the woods, even if we wanted to. Except when it rains. And I tend to believe the mashers stay home when it rains."

His eyebrows did their crinkling trick again. "Well, you might consider it. Pepper spray's also good for breaking up dog fights."

She followed his gaze toward Fleur. The Lab sat in the

kitchen doorway, her eyes wide, her tongue dripping dainty drops of drool in a silent plea for her overdue, after-walk dog biscuit. Destiny tried in vain to imagine her in a fight.

Daniel changed the subject. "There's not much more I can accomplish tonight, but I'll follow up on this tomorrow. Even if this perp walked out of the woods under his own power, from what you've said, he must have suffered some kind of head injury. I'll check the area hospitals and put in a word at the local clinics."

"Thank you." She discovered she meant it. "For your help."

His face softened in that slight smile again. "It's what I'm here for."

"And for believing me, that I was attacked and wasn't on drugs. I know I didn't make your job any easier, Detective."

"Daniel."

"Daniel."

The pause that followed reminded Destiny of the awkwardness of a first date. Standing in the doorway, wondering if the other person had enjoyed the evening, wondering how to say good-bye. A feeling very similar to the trepidation and anticipation that he might expect a kiss.

Destiny's gaze rested on Daniel's mouth, a strong line above an uncompromising chin. A good, firm mouth. She had to smother a giggle. It was time for a hot cup of tea and a good night's sleep.

"Destiny, I'm going to have to ask you again what you were doing out in the park tonight."

Apparently his thoughts had not wandered as far afield as hers had.

"It's a long, humiliating, and ultimately very boring story," she said, managing to maintain a sober, earnest expression. "Thoroughly irrelevant."

"Nothing is irrelevant to the investigation of an attempted homicide."

Despite the sympathy in his eyes, the words chilled her. "You might have to charge me for hitting him with my bat?"

His hand gripped her shoulder, steadying her. "I meant his attempting to kill you. Are you sure you're all right?"

She swallowed and managed a smile. "Just tired, I guess. I forgot that part."

He held her gaze. She hadn't noticed before how very blue his eyes were. "I haven't forgotten it. And I need to know as much as possible about what happened tonight to prevent it from happening again."

He released her shoulder to pull out his notebook.

"It was my sister's idea." Exhaustion almost outweighed her embarrassment. "She's gotten into New Agey stuff since her divorce. Astrology, tarot, crystals—things like that. But she's not a flake," Destiny added.

Daniel nodded, though his brows inched closer together.

"She's exploring her spirituality, and it's been really good for her."

"Just because I'm a cop doesn't mean I automatically assume people who wear crystals are flakes. Perhaps the shorter version of the story?"

"I thought you wanted every detail."

He smiled. "I was wrong."

It was a smile she couldn't help but return. "Serena thinks I need . . ." She was *not* going to tell Detective Parks her sister thought she needed a man. "She thinks my life is in a rut. She got the idea that this full moon was a critical time for me, and that if I went out and, well, basked in it, that I'd find a soul— that something positive would happen."

There. She hadn't died of embarrassment. And she'd told

almost the whole truth. She beamed at Daniel.

He blinked, letting his eyebrows relax back into place. "After your experiences in the park, I find it hard to imagine your life in a rut." He put away the notebook. "You won't mind if I hope it doesn't get any more exciting? That's all I need for tonight. Will you be all right here alone?"

"I'll be fine." Though she intended to turn on every light in the house after he left. "I've got Fleur with me."

His mouth hinted at a smile. "Don't forget to lock your doors. A lot of people around here don't, but it's a good idea. I may want you to come to the park in the daylight, to go over the sequence of events again, if you don't mind."

"Sure."

He stepped back off the stoop. "All right. I'll call you tomorrow."

"Good night." She managed to shut the door and throw the bolt before the giggles caught up with her. "Too bad this wasn't a date," she told Fleur, leaning on the door. "He'll actually call me. He has to. It's his job."

Fleur cocked her head and whined.

"Not that I'd want to date Detective Parks." She shrugged out of her jacket and tossed it over a chair. "Sure, he's attractive, in a rumpled kind of way. But he's too obsessive-compulsive, I can tell. And he thinks I'm a flake. Besides, I know you have your heart set on Officer Riggs."

She stepped into the kitchen, flicking on the gas under the teakettle. Fleur whined again.

"A sensible choice, too. Someone who loves you and brings you Twinkies. Forget all this moonlight and soul mate stuff, Fleur. From now on, I'm falling in love based on quantifiable criteria. Though I think I'll set my sights higher than Twinkies. If you have any other good advice, feel free to share."

She glanced down at her dog. Fleur's forehead wrinkled and her eyes glowed with the effort of passing along a desperately important message.

Destiny set down her teacup. "I'm sorry. You're right. I *did* forget your cookie."

So much for a quiet evening of taped baseball and microwaved leftovers. Daniel looked down at the blood welling from his finger and decided he could skip spaghetti for the evening. In fact, the sooner he went to bed, the sooner the day would be over.

He turned off the tap and grabbed the gauze pad he'd covered with antiseptic cream. He would have to buy Mrs. Thielsen a new tea towel—he'd left blood all over the one she'd loaned him while she'd searched through her files to check that her little D'Artagnan was current on all his vaccinations. It would have been the perfect end to the perfect day to find out he needed a series of rabies shots. But the savage beast wasn't due for a rabies booster for another year and a half.

At a shrill complaint from his housemate, he looked up from his wound.

"I know the kitty door's locked, Edgar. I don't want you going out tonight."

Amber eyes blinked up at Daniel from beside the kitchen door. Dangerous white teeth showed as the cat meowed his demand.

"Don't tempt me. There's a killer loose out there."

Edgar stretched his cream-and-chocolate-colored bulk, his claws kneading the mat beside the door, showing his contempt for his bitter rival and next-door nemesis.

"I don't mean D'Artagnan." Though the tiny teacup poodle had more spunk beneath that apricot fluff than Daniel

34

would have given him credit for.

Mrs. Thielsen had rushed out her front door as he'd driven up to his house that evening, shouting that a wolf was killing her dog. Daniel had grabbed the pepper spray from his glove compartment and rushed to Mrs. Thielsen's back gate.

When he'd seen blood on the muzzle of the snarling Chow mix that had invaded Mrs. Thielsen's yard, he'd feared the worst for little D'Artagnan. But the blood had been the intruder's own, the tiny poodle darting out from under the back porch to nip the bigger dog.

The pepper spray had distracted the snarling chow while Daniel grabbed D'Artagnan and dashed for Mrs. Thielsen's kitchen.

"I should have let the little devil take care of himself," Daniel muttered, wrapping adhesive bandages around the puncture wounds the excited D'Artagnan had inflicted on his fingers. "He was doing fine on his own."

In fact, given the events of the evening, Daniel was surprised he'd been able to be of any assistance at all. If Mrs. Thielsen had owned a baseball bat, she would have thought him about as heroic as Destiny Millbrook had.

He shook his head in disgust at himself. He hadn't become a police officer to impress anybody. But he couldn't keep his mind off skull fractures and baseball bats and what an intelligent woman like Destiny Millbrook had been doing traipsing through the redwoods after dark. Her story of basking in the moonlight was too absurd to be a lie, but he couldn't shake the feeling that she had been hiding something—her pauses and blushes would have tipped off a clueless rookie—and that bothered him.

If she had been meeting a boyfriend, if he had gotten rough and she had been forced to fight him off, why would she have lied? She couldn't have expected to hide the relationship when they'd found him.

He dismissed the unduly disturbing idea of Destiny Millbrook as a prostitute. No intelligent hooker would agree to meet a trick in the woods, and as attractive as Destiny was in a T-shirt and jeans, it was hardly come-on attire.

So, what *had* she been up to? He had the strangest feeling it would come back to haunt him.

Edgar hopped onto the counter and pushed his head under Daniel's arm, mewling softly.

"I called animal control about the stray, but I don't know whether they'll catch it tonight or not. You'll have to use the litter box." Daniel scratched the cat's ears before putting away his first-aid supplies.

Blank spots and loose ends bothered him. He had to keep his mind open to the possibility that Destiny was involved in something shady, even though it didn't seem likely—whatever she didn't want to tell him, his instincts doubted it pertained to the case.

Regardless, he had plenty of blank spots and loose ends to follow up in connection with County Supervisor Barclay's plane crash. There was no evidence of foul play at the moment. But still, the spectacular death of a prominent—and currently controversial—member of the political community took priority over a botched mugging attempt in the park.

Even if the victim had eyes the color and potency of strong-brewed Guatemalan coffee with a dash of pure cream.

A piercing yowl brought him back to reality. Edgar had given up on the kitty door and was padding down the hallway toward the bedroom.

"You're right. It's nearly one o'clock. That's what I get for rescuing dogs and damsels in distress."

Daniel stripped off his ruined shirt and pants on his way down the hall to the bathroom. By the time he had brushed his teeth, Edgar had claimed the center of his bed. Daniel managed to push his way under the covers, and Edgar curled up in his spot against Daniel's back.

"It still bothers me," Daniel confessed to the cat as he clicked off the lamp by the bed. "She wasn't doing drugs. If she'd known her attacker, she'd have told us, especially since she expected us to find him. What could she be hiding and why?"

Like an inspiration, her description of her walk came back to him. What had she meant by *basking* in the moonlight? Had she intended to bask nude? He felt the pleasant click of puzzle pieces falling into place. That would certainly account for her embarrassment.

He grinned and shook his head.

" 'Night, Edgar." Satisfied, he burrowed his head into his pillow and let the darkness take his thoughts.

As usual, it took only minutes for Daniel to fall asleep. But he did not sleep with his usual soundness, and he awoke in the morning with the same image haunting his mind as when he'd drifted to sleep—the image of Destiny Millbrook's trim body bathed in the soft rays of the full moon.

Chapter 3

The anguished cry of the telephone ripped Destiny out of a land of threatening dreams and the comfort of a low, masculine voice. Her hand found the receiver, but she couldn't force her eyes open far enough to see what time it was. She hadn't expected Detective Parks to call before nine.

"Daniel?" she mumbled, pushing up her eyelids with her free hand. Seven-fifteen.

"Daniel?" The feminine voice that responded held far too much pep for so early on a Saturday morning. "My, my. Who's Daniel, Desty? Judging from your tone, I'd guess he's tall, dark, and handsome."

Destiny let her eyes fall closed once more. "No, Serena, he's not. He's tall, medium-tan, and anal-retentive. He's a police detective."

"Law enforcement," her sister drawled, undeterred. "A definite change for you. Change is good." Serena purred with self-satisfaction. "You tried it, didn't you? You went out and let the power of the full moon flow through you, charging your primal femininity, and you met a man. Don't thank me now. You can wait until the wedding."

"As a matter of fact, Reenie, I did meet a man in the park." Destiny sat up, her free hand moving to the bruises on her neck. "He tried to kill me."

"A *policeman* tried to *kill* you?"

"No, the policeman drove me to the hospital afterward."

"The hospital?" Serena gasped. "Oh, my God, baby, are you all right? What happened?"

Destiny's annoyance disappeared at her sister's distress.

38

"I'm fine, Reenie. Some guy grabbed me, and I hit him with my baseball bat."

"But the police took you to the hospital."

"He left a couple of bruises on my neck, so—"

"Your neck!"

"They're no big deal, Reenie, really. The doctor said to take two aspirin and not to bother calling him in the morning."

"Oh, my God. Somebody tried to strangle you. I'm coming over."

"Reenie—"

"I'll be there in five minutes."

"You're overreacting." But Destiny could already hear the dial tone. She set down the receiver with a sigh. Serena would blow the whole thing out of proportion. No doubt she'd spend the entire morning chanting over healing crystals and brewing tea for Destiny's throat. After goading her into this whole mess in the first place.

"Sisters," she observed to Fleur, who had one limpid brown eye focused on Destiny from her spot by the bedroom door. "You can't live with them; you can't kill them."

But her sister's concern wrapped about her like a favorite old afghan as she clambered out of bed and stumbled to the bathroom. No one knew her better than Serena did.

And no one knew Serena better than she did.

She pulled off her nightshirt and dropped it on the bathroom floor. Five minutes for Serena usually meant forty-five; in a crisis like this, Destiny estimated she had at least fifteen minutes for a shower.

The overstuffed, silver-striped sofa appeared to swallow Fiona Barclay whole. She sat ramrod straight in its center in her trim black dress, looking like a collection of bones and skin with no stuffing of her own. Her brother, Philip Brooks, sat beside her, his long, narrow hands wrapped around hers.

Looking at them together, no one could have failed to see the family resemblance. The angel-blond hair, fine-boned features, and stubborn chins matched them like a brace of fine greyhounds. They even shared the same dark circles under their clear green eyes.

Gage Barclay's death was no longer Daniel's official concern, and today was supposed to be his day off, but he'd known Fiona for almost twenty years, and she and Daniel's ex-wife were golfing partners. He couldn't leave it to a stranger to bring her the latest news.

"Pilot error?" she repeated, her words brittle as frost.

"That's the preliminary finding of the FAA investigator," Daniel said, his professional detachment not quite protecting him from her pain. "It looks as if Gage may have run into some bad wind sheer and overcompensated."

"The wind *was* gusting off the ocean yesterday. It didn't die down until nearly six," Philip said, his voice aching for his sister. "Anyone can have a lapse—"

"Gage was a good pilot," Fiona objected. Daniel could see her hands shaking in her lap.

"Of course he was," Philip agreed. "Good enough to think he could fly when he probably shouldn't have."

"They're not saying he was negligent in any way," Daniel broke in. "The slightest error in adjustment in a situation like that can be fatal. The coroner says Gage died instantly, Fiona. He didn't suffer."

"No, suffering is left to the rest of us." She shook off her brother's hand and stood. "Don't treat me as if I'm about to fall apart, Philip. I can't bear it. It just reminds me . . ." She stopped, clasping her fluttering hands together. "Can I get you a drink, Daniel?"

His gaze met Philip's, and the worry he saw there mirrored his own. "No, thank you, Fiona." He stood. "I have another call to make, and—"

"Wait, Daniel, please." She crossed to an antique tea table, where a bottle of fine brandy sat, and poured a small glass. She drank it in a single swallow. "Medicinal purposes. My hands won't stop shaking."

She crossed her arms and looked from Daniel to Philip and back again. "You both believe that, don't you? That Gage got himself killed acting like an irresponsible boy."

Daniel winced at the raw pain in her eyes. He sat back down. If yelling at him would give Fiona a measure of emotional release, the least he could do was allow her the opportunity.

But she didn't yell. Her voice was shaking too much for that. "Pilot error did not cause Gage's crash. I don't care what the FAA says. Somebody sabotaged that plane. Gage was murdered."

He would have preferred yelling.

Philip stood and moved toward his sister. "Fee, honey, don't make this worse than it is."

She brushed him away, her eyes shiny and fierce. "I'm not out of my head with grief, Philip, and I'm not going to shut up and be a good little girl." She turned on Daniel. "Doesn't it strike you as suspicious that three nights ago Gage announced he was going to cast the deciding vote against the ShopSmart development project and yesterday his plane crashed minutes after takeoff?"

Daniel kept his expression calm. "Fiona, there's no evidence of—"

"It doesn't matter who they get to replace him on the Board of Supervisors." She started pacing back and forth in front of the tea table. "You know Eddie Bedrosian only had the guts to stand up to the developers because of Gage. Salton Enterprises is going to get that agricultural land rezoned, and we're going to be led by our noses into the strip mall century. Who benefits?"

She didn't wait for an answer. "Salton Enterprises benefits, that's for sure, and what's-his-name the corporate shark from ShopSmart, and that Geary woman Philip represents, the one who owns the land. For starters."

"Fiona," Philip said.

"Gage had been receiving threats." She pushed a fist to her mouth, blinked, and continued. "On the phone. Here and at his office."

"He didn't tell me that," her brother said. "As his partner, I should have known." Philip ran the law office Gage Barclay had temporarily deserted when he was elected county supervisor.

"He didn't tell anyone. He didn't want to give those bastards the satisfaction of thinking he was scared."

"Fiona . . ." Daniel wanted to help her understand that her husband had died in a senseless accident with no one to blame. He couldn't find the words. He should have become a marine biologist, as his mother had wanted.

"Did you get any of these threats on tape?" His voice sounded discouraging, but he couldn't help that.

"Yes." She gave him the ghost of a triumphant smile— probably her first smile in twenty-four hours.

Daniel could have kicked himself.

Philip frowned at him. "Look, Fee, just let it go."

"And let them get away with murder?"

"There was no murder, Fiona," Daniel said.

Her lips thinned with determination, though her eyes glistened with unshed tears. "What about the threats, then?

That's got to be against the law. Intimidating a public official."

"If you want me to be honest with you, Fiona, there's not much the police can do about it now. Even if we connect the threats with a particular person, the tapes probably won't be admissible in court. But give them to me, and I'll listen to them." He knew he'd regret the offer, but he couldn't let her think no one cared. By the time he got back to her to tell her the threats were mere spite and not connected to her husband's death, maybe she'd be ready to hear it.

"Thanks, Danny." She gave him another smile, this one so brave it almost broke his heart. Philip reached for her, and she leaned into him. "Protecting that land and the merchants of Hope Point was important to Gage. I can't let the developers win just because he died."

"We understand," Philip assured her.

"No, you don't." Fiona brushed a hand across her eyes before looking up at her brother. "You agreed to represent Pleasance Geary when she decided to sell that land. You told Gage you thought the ShopSmart development would be good for the local economy."

"I still think so. That doesn't mean I can't understand your feelings."

Fiona frowned at him. "Don't patronize me. You think grief is making me irrational."

"Who said you were rational before?" Philip teased, receiving an elbow in the side for his trouble. But Fiona's eyes warmed a little.

She turned to Daniel. "I'll bring the tapes to the station this afternoon. Gage kept them at his office."

"Fine."

"Thanks, Daniel," Philip added, an arm still around his sister.

"Don't thank me yet. There's probably nothing I can do. I'll see myself out." He made his way back through the foyer and out onto the steep circular drive where he'd left his unmarked car. The homes along Redwood Hill Road all had sweeping vistas of Hope Point and the bay to go along with their vaulted ceilings, hot tubs, and BMWs.

He reflected that when most of the crimes a detective investigated involved indigent dope addicts and troubled kids, he could forget that the homes on the hill sheltered their own tragedies.

Looking up at the towering redwoods surrounding the gracefully luxurious house, Daniel wondered if the Barclays ever got nervous during windstorms.

A low growl stopped his hand as he reached for the car door. Lunch. He'd forgotten all about it. He glanced at his watch. No time now. He had two more doctors' offices to call before he dropped by Destiny Millbrook's.

No problem. He climbed into the front seat of the department's old Chevy and wrenched the ignition with more force than was necessary. He didn't have to eat. Helping damsels in distress was fulfilling enough.

But any more distressed damsels who crossed his path were going to have to fend for themselves. With their baseball bats and pit bull tenacity, they probably didn't need him anyway.

"You need help. Admit it."

Destiny set her screwdriver down on top of the stepladder and removed the light bulb from between her teeth. "Here, hold this. That would help."

Without moving from her position leaning against the kitchen counter, Serena stretched out a hand and took the bulb. The manicured nails of her other hand ticked against her cup of ginger tea. "You could kill yourself climbing around on that old ladder."

"You could hold it steady for me." Destiny continued to work on the light fixture.

Serena rested a hand on one rickety wooden rung. "I'm not always here to look out for you, Desty. You need a man."

"To change a light bulb?" The last recalcitrant screw loosened and dropped on Serena's head.

"Apparently so." Her sister handed her the good bulb and bent down to retrieve the screw.

"What kind of idiot would put in a light fixture you have to use a screwdriver on, anyway?" Destiny asked. Holding the glass globe in one hand, she replaced the old bulb. She glanced into the globe. "Ick, there are dead things in there." She quickly placed it over the bare bulb and began working on the screws.

"Some people would take this opportunity to clean that," Serena commented without much hope.

Destiny glanced at her sister. Serena would scrub it to a shine. And it showed. Her long, glossy, chestnut hair was pulled back in a neat ponytail. Her black scoop-neck shirt and ironed chinos accentuated her curves while showing off her jazzercised body. She looked like a model for J. Crew.

Destiny doubted a casual observer would guess they were sisters, despite the resemblance in features. Her own hair hadn't relaxed from the "impossible to get wrong" home perm she'd tried last week. Her T-shirt had punctures on one side from Fleur's tug-of-war with it, though she'd hidden them under a faded blue denim shirt what's-his-name had left behind in his hurried move to Arizona. The holey T-shirt also accessorized nicely with her jeans that had one knee ripped out.

"You know what I mean," Serena said as Destiny climbed down the sagging ladder rungs to safety. "This place could use a man's touch. And so could you."

"Serena, Susan B. Anthony just rolled over in her grave."

Her sister shrugged, following Destiny and the ladder out the back door toward the tool shed. "I'm not saying it's like needing spiritual fulfillment or needing a purpose to your life. Or even like needing chocolate when you're PMS-ing. But men do come in handy from time to time."

"I'm sure Jesse would be thrilled to know he ranks somewhere below chocolate on your necessities-of-life scale," Destiny commented, hoping to steer the topic away from her own love life—or lack thereof—to her sister's new romance. It almost worked.

Serena's expression softened, showing a hint of innocent warmth Destiny hadn't seen in her sister in too many years. "That's different. When you find someone so right—so right it's scary—then it isn't even really need anymore. It's just a part of you." She opened the shed door. "It was never this way with David. Not even when I was desperately in love with him and thought it was forever. Now that I know what love's really like, I know there's someone out there for you, too."

"Hence the 'moonlight madness, man of your dreams' stuff." Destiny settled the ladder into place and grabbed her V-forked weeder from its spot underneath the used sandpaper.

"That was a stupid idea." Serena fingered the quartz crystal that hung on a silver chain around her neck. "I don't know what I would have done if anything had happened to you. I'm so, so sorry."

"I'm the one who went out there." Destiny resisted the impulse to touch her own throat. The night before had warped and stretched into the memory of a bad dream. Only the occasional painful swallow or her sister's reminders brought back the reality of it, the terror.

Serena followed her across the lawn to the one tiny patch of the backyard that got enough sun to grow vegetables. Fleur had dug up the carrots—the dog loved carrots—but the cherry tomatoes and snow peas looked healthy.

A brief, sharp yearning for her garden in Sacramento pierced her. Peppers, corn, eggplant. Sunshine. And real tomatoes that would turn red before the rain split and rotted them. She inhaled the good smell of damp earth and green plants and smiled at her cherry tomatoes. If she wanted anything bigger, she could always go to the Farmer's Market, and in Hope Point she never needed air conditioning.

"Maybe you'll have to wait to meet your soul mate," Serena was saying, interrupting her garden reverie. "But that doesn't mean you have to be alone. If we weren't in love, I think Jesse and I could base a relationship on the fact that he fixes my leaky faucets and I feed him home-cooked meals."

"I can fix my own leaky faucets, and I hate cooking."

"Every time Sarah comes to visit you, she comes home on a sugar high from all the cookies and pies and heaven knows what other diabetic-coma-inducing confections you've made."

"That's baking. Not cooking." Destiny wrenched out a stubborn dandelion. "Speaking of my niece . . ."

"I know what you're going to say, Desty, but we can't tell her what happened. You know how she is."

Destiny sat back on her heels. "She's twelve years old. Old enough to know the truth."

"She'll blame herself."

Destiny almost smiled. "Just like her mom does?"

"I'm mature enough to cope with my self-imposed guilt-trips, thank you very much," Serena said, drawing herself up.

"Sarah still blames herself for David and I divorcing, for heaven's sake."

"I'm the one who went out in the park by myself after sunset," Destiny pointed out again. She was starting to sound like Officer Riggs. "No one else is responsible for my actions. Sarah's going to see the bruises, Reenie, and she's going to ask what happened. She'll want to know the results of the moonlight experiment, even if she doesn't believe in star charts and soul mates."

"You're right." Serena pulled one of Destiny's flyaway curls. "But she's still so afraid of losing the people she cares about . . ."

"So we give her the upbeat version." Destiny waved her weeder in a careless gesture. "Auntie Dess fighting crime with her trusty baseball bat and her not-so-trusty sidekick, Superfleur."

Serena frowned. "Next time, get a Rottweiler."

Destiny put her hands over her ears. "Hush. And don't you dare repeat that in front of Fleur."

Serena sighed, a long-suffering sigh. "When have either you or Fleur ever listened to me? You refuse to buy vegetables in the store—it would be cheaper at this point. You refuse to meet a nice man and forget wretched old what's-his-name, Alain. And now I find out you've never even cracked open those wonderful cookbooks I gave you for Christmas last year."

Destiny turned back to her weeding. "If you're so into cooking, you can make us lunch while I get something useful done."

Instead, Serena leaned over and plucked a snow pea off one of the vines. "You don't have to worry about being useful, Desty; you already are. You've got this place so fixed up the landlord is sure to raise the rent when you leave. You work in a library, for heaven's sake—anyone who can cheerfully help someone hunt down 'that poem about lutefisk I loved as a child' must be a saint. And I'll never be able to repay you for all you've done for me and Sarah."

"I'm here for you and Sarah because I love you. Well, because you're family."

"Ha, ha." Serena crunched another pea. "You need to get out and enjoy yourself. I'm not saying you need to jump in and get married. Don't worry about commitment yet. Just have some fun."

"I was in a relationship like that. I have no desire to repeat the experience." Destiny jabbed her weeder into the dirt rather more savagely than she'd intended.

"No, what's-his-name was in a relationship like that. That was the problem. You weren't. For you, everything is for keeps."

Destiny squinted at her sister. "You can't have it both ways. It's either moonlight or moonshine, not both. And after last night, it may be awhile before I make an effort to meet any man at all."

Serena tossed Destiny's pile of weeds toward the compost heap. "That bastard. I still think you ought to see Callista, have a tarot reading. She can cleanse you of the negativity of the attack better than I did."

"Thanks, Reenie." Destiny attacked another dandelion. "But I don't need a tarot reading. I don't need my spirit cleansed. And I don't need a man. Except maybe Daniel Parks. It would make me feel better if he caught the guy who grabbed me."

"How was it you described this delectable Daniel?" Serena asked, her voice speculative. "Tall, sun-kissed, and handsome?"

Destiny snorted. "I think 'anal-retentive' was the word I used."

"Well," Serena drawled, "that's not something I can tell from this angle. But there's something about this guy that shouts 'law enforcement.' Am I right?"

"Yes, ma'am," a distinctly male voice agreed. "Detective Daniel Parks. I hope it was all right to come through the back gate. No one answered the doorbell."

Destiny whispered a small, impolite word to her snow peas.

"I'm Serena Davis, Destiny's sister."

"A pleasure to meet you. Ms. Millbrook?"

Destiny forced a smile to her lips before pushing herself to her feet and turning around. Maybe he'd attribute her red face to the strain of weeding. "Destiny, remember? I'm sorry you had to hunt me down. I thought I could hear the bell out here."

"No problem. I noticed you'd retrieved your car from the park, so I thought you must be around here somewhere." His hard-angled face expressed detached competence—the air of "law-enforcement" Serena had noticed—but a smile lurked in his eyes. He'd definitely heard the "anal-retentive" remark.

"Why don't we go inside?" Destiny brushed her palms off on her jeans and led the way toward the back door.

Catching sight of her reflection in the kitchen window, she winced. Maybe he hadn't heard anything. Her appearance alone could account for his amusement. She wished she had taken a little more time choosing her wardrobe that morning.

But after seeing him last night in his wrinkled dress shirt and generic slacks with the grass stains on the knees, she hadn't expected him to show up in a forest-green henley and close-cut twill pants. And she certainly hadn't expected him to look so good in them.

She went straight to the sink to scrub the dirt from under

her fingernails. Thank heavens Serena had insisted on washing the week's worth of dirty dishes on the counter before brewing the aura-cleansing tea she'd brought over.

A thunder roll of thumping and scraping accompanied Fleur's emergence from her place under the tiny kitchen table. She immediately showered her undying devotion on the one person least likely to reciprocate it. But Destiny noted that Daniel favored her with a quick scratch behind the ears before Serena grabbed her collar and dragged her back.

"Down!" Serena's stern look dropped Fleur faster than Destiny's ever had. "Good girl. Now, Detective Parks—"

"Daniel's fine."

"Daniel."

Destiny winced. Serena was practically purring.

"Destiny and I were just about to fix ourselves some lunch. Would you like to join us?"

Daniel hesitated. "That's all right, I—"

"You haven't eaten yet, have you?" Serena interrupted.

Destiny watched as his official law enforcement expression melted away with his smile. "Was it the haunted, I'm-starving look in my eyes that gave me away?"

Serena laughed. "No, it was the way your pupils dilated when I mentioned food. All we've got is stuff for sandwiches. At least, I think we've got that much. You do have bread that isn't green, don't you, Desty?"

"Very funny," Destiny said, but she surreptitiously checked the loaf of wheat bread she pulled off the top of the fridge before handing it to her sister. "I just don't know if there's anything to put on it."

She opened the fridge door. "I know I have peanut butter—I keep it around to give Fleur her worm pills in." *Just what he wanted to know before lunch.* "But I don't have much jelly left."

She rummaged through the bottom drawers, hoping against reason to find a miraculous stash of sliced ham and cheese or a container of hummus with an expiration date in the right decade. "Lettuce, spinach, green beans." At least her vegetables were always fresh. "And some tomatoes and eggplant."

"Don't you even have any eggs for egg salad?" Serena asked.

Destiny shook her head. "Here's some mozzarella, a thing of cream cheese. And some . . . blue cheese? Eww. No." She tossed the old block of jack into the trash.

"Sorry," Serena said. "I'm afraid I spoke too soon."

Destiny rose from her crouch to find that Daniel had moved close behind her. His hand on the refrigerator door trapped her between him and the counter, but he didn't appear to notice. He was peering intently into the fridge.

She could smell his aftershave. Clean, not too spicy. The sun crinkles around his eyes looked even sexier up close.

"It looks like you've got all the fixings for an exceptional grilled eggplant sandwich. If you've got some olive oil?"

His eyes shone a deeper blue when he wasn't thinking about crime. And they were focused on her. Waiting for her to say something . . .

"Uh, sure. I've got olive oil." She pointed to the cupboard above the microwave.

Destiny met Serena's eyes across the broad expanse of Daniel's back. Her sister smiled like a cat.

"Great." Daniel spun the turntable in the cupboard until he found the oil. "We just need to toast the bread and . . . Where do you keep your frying pans? Oh, got one." He pulled the skillet from the drain board and flipped on a burner.

"I'm sorry." He flipped off the burner, his cheeks reddening. "Meet my alter ego, the Frugal Gourmet. I picked up cooking as a hobby a couple of years ago. It's a good stress reliever."

"Divorced?" Serena asked. Destiny shot her a look.

Daniel smiled. "You got me. It was learn to cook or eat out of a microwave for the rest of my life. Would you like your kitchen back now, Ms. Millbrook?"

"No." Destiny dropped the eggplant onto the counter beside him.

"You don't mind?"

"I don't see anyone else volunteering to grill eggplant."

He smiled sheepishly. "All right." He turned the burner back on and dragged out the cutting board from under the toaster.

That's when Destiny saw the punctures marring his fingers.

"What happened to your hand?" Without thinking, she grabbed it, just as she would have if he'd been Sarah or Serena. "You've been bitten. Cat bite?"

"Dog."

"Any bite is germy. Did you put antiseptic on it? I've got a first-aid kit in that drawer over there, Reenie, behind the light bulbs and potholders."

"I put antiseptic on it." His amused voice sounded awfully close again.

Destiny looked down at their hands, his fingers broad against hers, the knuckles scraped, the nails almost square. A strong hand. A very male hand.

"May I have it back?"

Destiny managed not to blush. She picked up the eggplant and slapped it into his palm. "I have a policy against biting the hand that feeds me, but I can see how you might have pushed a dog to it."

"Destiny!" Serena's look was quelling. "Daniel probably

got that bite in the line of duty. Did you have to fight off a drug dealer's pit bull?"

"Actually, it was a poodle."

"A standard poodle?" Serena tried.

"Teacup."

His gaze met Destiny's, and she realized his sense of humor had once more surprised her.

"I can see it biting your ankles," she said, risking Serena's wrath, "but your fingers? Were you trying to paw-cuff it?"

"I was saving the beastly little dog's life, if you must know."

"Ah!" Serena pounced, back in her element. "A hero as well as a chef! How are you with leaky faucets?" She smiled at her sister.

Daniel's eyebrows scrunched in confusion for the first time that afternoon. "Leaky faucets? I can't help you with that. The faucet in my kitchen is threatening to drive me out of my mind."

"What a coincidence." Serena's eyes narrowed like those of a cat watching a caged bird. "That just happens to be one of Destiny's areas of expertise. I'm sure she'd be more than happy to install a new washer or whatever in exchange for this incredible meal you're fixing. Isn't that right, Desty?"

If Serena *had* been a cat, there would have been canary feathers stuck all over her tongue.

Chapter 4

The afternoon wind whipping off the ocean ruffled the tops of the redwood trees, but, down below, their protection created a pocket of serenity broken only by the shouts of unseen children on the playground and the rumble of an occasional truck on the distant highway. The bitter, earthy scent of ferns mingled with the hint of salt tang from the sea.

The crunch of gravel beneath his loafers sounded discordant to Daniel's ears, out of sync with the hushed softness of the forest. His office was less than two hundred yards from this very spot, and it seemed like another world.

Fleur dodged across his path, the big Lab's nose straining at some fascinating scent just beyond the trail. She stopped abruptly, bringing Daniel to a halt as well, trapped behind her leash.

"Sorry." Destiny traded sides of the path with Daniel. "Fleur! Let's go!"

So far, Fleur was the only dog he'd seen on a leash in the park. Off the main streets, the leash law was not a high priority with Hope Point law enforcement. But he'd asked Destiny to bring Fleur along on the minuscule chance the dog's behavior might give them a clue about what had happened the night before. Fleur had to stay close enough to be observed.

He didn't expect anything tangible to come from the experiment. He didn't expect anything tangible from this whole expedition. But seeing the scene in the daylight would give him a better feel for the action of the night before and might jog something interesting from Destiny's memory.

He glanced at the woman walking beside him; her wild curls half-tamed by a red hair band, her cheeks brightened by the fresh air. It occurred to him just how long it had been since he'd walked in the woods with an attractive woman.

Grimly, he forced his mind back to business. He should have known better than to have lunch with Destiny and her sister. He had known better. But he'd managed to convince himself it was his stomach that had betrayed him—until he'd found himself zeroing in on the way Destiny licked the warm cream cheese oozing from her sandwich off her fingers.

The memory caused him to miss a step.

"Fleur? Yuck! Leave it!"

He ignored the brief scuffle between Destiny and her dog. He didn't want to know.

"The gazebo isn't much farther," he said. "When did you first start to hear voices?"

Destiny slowed, her fine features focused in thought. "I don't know. I got the feeling the men I heard must have been arguing for a while, but I didn't really notice it until I got almost to where I could see the gazebo. They raised their voices then."

"But you couldn't make out the words."

"I wasn't paying attention to that. I just wanted to slip past without disturbing them. It seemed to me they were arguing about money. At least, one of them said something like, 'You owe me, and you're going to make good on it.' And the other man said something about how that wasn't what they'd agreed on. I don't know."

She shook her head in frustration. "It's all fuzzy now. Talking about it, it sounds as if it could have been some kind of drug deal, but that didn't occur to me at the time. Probably because they didn't sound the way I'd expect drug dealers to sound. Not dangerous, you know? For some reason, I

56

thought they were talking about railroads."

"Were there other cars in the parking lot when you arrived?" He was pleased to note his mind remained on the case, not on the way she nibbled her lip as she thought.

"Five or six, I think. I'd been playing with Fleur in the soccer field for a while before we walked. The sun was setting when I entered the trees, but it wasn't dark yet. I could hear kids playing, not wanting to go home." She glanced at him. "It didn't seem dangerous."

The thought of Destiny Millbrook wandering into the woods after sundown without so much as a flashlight made his stomach clench, so he kept his mouth shut. Crime rarely touched the park—beyond the predictable rowdiness during Octoberfest—but for a single woman to walk in a secluded area after dark . . . At least her sense of self-preservation was developed enough that she hadn't left the bat in the car.

The gauzy scarf she'd put on before leaving her house hid the worst of the bruises on her neck, but he knew the position of each one. If—when—he caught the man who'd put them there, the perp would have reason to be grateful Daniel was bound by his duty as a police officer not to kill the guy.

"Daniel?" A male voice. "Hello again."

Daniel tried not to look as though Philip Brooks had materialized out of thin air on the path before him. So much for concentrating on his job.

"Philip! I'm surprised to run into you here."

"I might say the same." The man's green eyes narrowed with mischief. "I thought you rushed off this morning to work, and here I find you out taking a stroll in the park with a lovely young woman." He caught Fleur's muzzle just in time to keep the Lab from pressing her wet nose against his ecru slacks. "And her lovely dog."

"Fleur, sit. Sit!" Destiny smiled apologetically at Philip,

and he smiled back, the same dazzling smile Daniel remembered from high school when he'd envied the older boy's easy charm and his effect on attractive women.

"Don't I know you from somewhere?" Philip asked Destiny. He glanced at Daniel. "Aren't you going to introduce us?"

"No," Daniel said amiably, pleased to be able to deflect Philip's charisma from this particular attractive woman. "As a matter of fact, I'm conducting police business."

"Tough job."

"Someone's got to do it."

Philip laughed. "Fine. If that's the way you want to be about it. I'll talk to you later, Danny." His face sobered. "I dropped Fiona's tapes off at the station for you. I doubt there's anything worthwhile on them, but it means a lot to her to have you investigate."

"I'll listen to them this evening if I can."

"If you do find out who made the calls, even if there's no connection to—" He glanced at Destiny. "—anything else— I'd still like to know. Something should be done about it. My client obviously wants the development to move forward, but I know Mrs. Geary would agree that the project should be delayed if there's any question of ethical problems on the part of anyone involved. Of course, I wouldn't want to tell her the delay was my fault until after I made sure her shotgun wasn't loaded."

"I'll keep that in mind," Daniel assured him.

"Thanks." Philip started past them, but as he moved by Destiny, he stopped. "Got it!" He turned that dazzling smile back on her. "The library. You work at the county library, right?"

Destiny nodded, and Daniel tried not to show his surprise. *A librarian?*

"I knew you looked familiar. I was in there the other day."
Her forehead wrinkled. "I don't remember you."

And she would, Daniel thought. Any woman still
breathing would remember Philip Brooks if he smiled at her.

"I didn't check anything out," Philip said. "Just looked at
some old county records on microfiche. Boring stuff. Next
time I'll be sure to stop by and say hello." He raised his eyebrows at Daniel in triumph and turned down the path.

"You're a librarian?" Daniel asked, because that seemed
safer than recommending she steer clear of smooth-talking
lawyers.

"My friends call me Marian." Her voice was dark. "You
think I ought to put my hair in a bun and wear wire-rimmed
glasses?"

"No." Daniel moved once more up the path. "It's just that
after seeing your kitchen this afternoon, I find it hard to picture you letting your life be regulated by the Dewey Decimal
system."

He'd certainly taken her attention off Philip Brooks. Her
eyes sparked at him. "If you have a decent memory, you don't
need a system. I know where everything in my kitchen is. Of
course, that wouldn't be practical if I had three hundred
people traipsing through my house every day."

"Or if you had a hundred thousand kitchen implements."
She almost smiled. "Exactly."

They passed around the huge stump of a redwood tree cut
for lumber over a hundred years before, and Daniel saw the
white latticework of the gazebo through the trees up ahead.

"As a lesser mortal who craves order, you'll forgive me if I
take a few notes?" He pulled out his notebook and flipped it
open. "You said you were going to take another path, but
Fleur ran ahead?"

"Yes, the one that branches off between the gazebo and

the creek. I'll show you when we get there. I was on that path from the parking lot—" She pointed to it as they stepped into the gazebo clearing. "—not this one from the road. I meant to turn east. Fleur went straight north."

Fleur tugged Destiny toward the gazebo.

"She started snuffling in the azaleas," Destiny continued, as Fleur demonstrated, her tail thrashing behind her.

"What's she got there?" Daniel asked, pushing aside thick clumps of green leaves.

"I generally prefer not to find out," Destiny warned, but Daniel forced his way into the bushes until he could see Fleur's head again. He pushed her nose aside and gingerly picked up the aluminum foil she'd found.

"Burrito wrapping. Just think, a couple classes in forensic detection, and you could be having this much fun." A garbage can sat not fifteen feet away. Keeping his littering lecture to himself, he disposed of the foil.

"I see the whole diabolical plan," Destiny mused, following him around the path toward the gazebo's entrance. "A ring of muggers who lure unsuspecting citizens to their doom by tossing out bait to their dogs. But last night their plans went awry, because they were fighting over the last bite of chicken burrito. Am I ready to make detective?"

"Don't quit your day job." He was relieved to hear her joking. Even in the daylight, this couldn't be easy.

As he reached the steps up to the gazebo, a bouquet of lilies appeared in the archway and almost ran him over.

"Excuse me." He stepped back, stumbling over Fleur.

The lilies dropped a foot, revealing a receding hairline and a pair of harried dark eyes. "Look, I'm sorry, but you can't use the gazebo today. We're trying to set up for a wedding here. We're asking everyone to stay out of our way."

"This won't take more than five minutes," Daniel said

with an assurance that usually had a calming effect on people. The lilies lowered another six inches, showing the man's lips, stretched in a tight line of frustration. "Forget it, buddy. Go whisper in your girlfriend's ear somewhere else. I've got a baby grand piano to maneuver into this place."

Introducing himself as a police officer often had a dampening effect on Daniel's social relations. But sometimes he couldn't help enjoying it.

"Detectivel Parks, Hope Point PD." He held his badge above the flowers to give the man a good view. "Five minutes, I promise."

The lily-man's eyes closed in an expression of tragedy. "Go ahead. Do what you want. What do I care?" The bouquet bobbed down the stairs, its bearer sighing behind it.

The interior of the gazebo did not live up to the promise of romance given by the outside. The ivy entwining the latticework served only to create a grotto-like gloom. The utilitarian cement floor and a quartet of wrought-iron benches didn't provide much hope for finding hidden clues, either. A hastily set-up wooden altar stood against the east wall. Daniel hoped the flower man's skill could transform the gazebo so it didn't look so much like the setting for a pagan sacrifice.

"What are we looking for?" Destiny asked.

"I don't know," Daniel admitted. "But we'd better find something to do for five minutes. I'd hate to disappoint that guy by leaving early. Do you have any idea where in the gazebo those men were standing?"

She moved toward the southernmost bench. "Over here, near where Fleur was snuffling outside in the bushes."

Currently, Fleur showed little interest in the area, having found an old strawberry ice cream stain on the cement.

"Those men probably didn't have anything to do with what happened to me," Destiny said as Daniel moved beside

61

her. "There were two of them, and only one man attacked me. And I didn't hear anyone following me after I dragged Fleur away from here."

"I understand." Daniel scanned the bench and the floor beneath it. "But even if they're not involved, if we can locate those men, they might have heard or seen something that could help us find your attacker."

He knelt down on the cement. A couple of gum wrappers and some dead ivy leaves were his only reward. "I suppose it was too much to hope for that one of them would have dropped a business card."

"What's that?" Destiny pointed to the latticed wall just above the bench.

"Ivy?"

"No." She leaned over the bench. "Here."

He pushed himself to his feet beside her and followed her hand to a cluster of ivy leaves. Something glittered beneath them.

"Careful," he warned. "If it falls down into that ivy, we'll never get it out."

Destiny cupped her hands beneath the leaves as he reached for the shiny object, but the bit of metal stuck tightly to the vine. Daniel had to rip the strand of ivy away from the wall before he could pull the item free. A weak ray of sunlight winked off a narrow silver clip. Diamond chips outlined one side of the S-curved sliver of mother-of-pearl that decorated it.

"A money clip," Destiny said. Her fingers tickled his palm like feathers as she turned the clip over. "I don't see any identifying marks on it."

The least movement would have brushed his arm against her shoulder. He could smell the scent of roses in her hair. He didn't step away.

"Someone probably lost it during a wedding last weekend. I'll put a note in the classifieds." He slipped the clip into his pants pocket. "So much for the gazebo. I want to move on to where you were attacked. Are you up to that?"

Her eyes met his with an expression he couldn't interpret. "I want to help. I don't want this guy free to hurt other people."

Last night, when the perp had attacked her, she'd shown quick thinking and bravery. Since then she'd had time to acknowledge the terror of what had happened, and she was still facing it head on. He resisted the urge to reach out and touch her; it was not his place to offer comfort.

"We don't have many leads in this case, Destiny. Unless this guy shows up at a hospital or clinic, it may be difficult to track him down. But I promise you I'll do my best to catch him."

"I know you will."

And then he realized what was different about her eyes. The skepticism was gone. At least for this moment, she was putting her trust in him. Uncharacteristically, the knowledge rattled him.

As a police detective, he was accustomed to the extremes of reaction people had to his profession, from resentful distrust of anyone in authority to the awed belief he could pull off miracles of detection worthy of an episode of *Law and Order*.

The truth was that a quick police response and basic investigation skills solved most crimes in Hope Point. That and the fact that criminals were rarely as bright as they were portrayed on TV.

The police department in general, and Daniel in particular, had a good record for arrests and convictions in the cases the detective division investigated, from robbery and auto theft to rare instances of rape and homicide.

He gave each case his best, regardless of what the victims expected of him. But meeting Destiny's clear, dark eyes, he found he wanted to be worthy of her trust.

Which meant that at some point during the course of the afternoon he had lost his suspicions about the truthfulness of her story. Fine, if that was instinct speaking. Not so fine if it was his libido.

The voice of the flower man rescued him from his confused immobility. "Wait! You can't go in there. This is a gazebo, not Grand Central Station. Besides, you'll interrupt the policeman's tryst. Maybe I can get him to arrest you for trespassing."

Apparently the intruder heeded the warning, because it was the flower man who appeared in the entranceway, a piano stool in his hands. "Are you finished? The piano's here."

"It's all yours."

Daniel led Destiny and Fleur down the cement steps and along the path around the gazebo. Movement caught his eye from down the path toward the street; a glimpse of a gray suit and gray felt hat. Something about the sight struck him as strange, beyond the oddity of someone wearing a suit and hat in the park on a Saturday, but the figure was gone before he could determine what bothered him about it. Perhaps it was that something about the person seemed familiar, even from the back.

He smiled wryly. How many people did he know who wore suits? Lots of them. He knew most of the lawyers in Jasper County, at least from the courtroom.

"Don't they have ambulances to chase?"

"What?" Destiny was staring at him.

"All the lawyers in the park today. I think I just saw another one."

"Your friend Philip is a lawyer, too?"

"Yes." *Smooth move, Parks. Bring the conversation back to Philip.* He continued along the path.

"I thought he might be when he said Pleasance was his client."

"Who?"

"Hideaway Hill."

"Hideaway Hill?" He wondered if her conversations would make more sense the longer he spent with her. "That actually sounds familiar."

"It should." She frowned at him. "The property ShopSmart wants to buy? They've had article after article on the project in the newspaper for the past six months. ShopSmart wants to buy Hideaway Hill, one of those ocean view cow pastures north of town, and build a superstore there, but the land is zoned for agriculture, and—"

"I know about the project," Daniel said. They left the gazebo clearing, stepping onto the path that led toward the creek and the parking lot. He noticed that Destiny's hair echoed the russet-brown of the redwood trees' bark.

"Some people think the project will bring in jobs and stimulate the economy," she continued. "I know Pleasance Geary, the woman who owns the land. Her granddaughter is on my softball team. She seems to believe the development will benefit the whole county—more tax revenues, I guess. I don't much like the idea of destroying the scenery with a big ugly warehouse, but mostly I worry about the local merchants. A store like that could force some of the downtown stores out of business, which would—"

"I know about the debate, too," Daniel interrupted, though he liked the way her hands waved when she talked with such animation.

"Yes? I couldn't be sure." She measured him with a look.

"After all, you don't read the newspaper, you don't frequent the library . . ."

"I listen to the news on the radio," he defended himself. "And I buy lots of books."

She didn't respond.

"From local downtown retailers, I might add."

He expected at least a hint of a smile, but she stopped abruptly, bringing Fleur to an undignified halt at the end of her leash.

"Destiny?" Daniel hesitated. He hadn't said anything that could have offended her; he felt almost certain of it. "Is something wrong?"

She turned to him, and her face looked pinched. "No. Sorry. I just had the strangest feeling. . . ." She glanced back the way they had come. "I thought I heard someone behind us."

She shook her head. "Paranoia, I guess. I didn't think I'd feel this jumpy."

"It's understandable." He let himself briefly rest a hand on her shoulder as they moved forward again. "But I don't think you have anything to worry about. No one's going to jump two healthy adults walking a dog Fleur's size."

She smiled, and warmth returned to her eyes. "But I feel so vulnerable without my bat."

"Erstwhile softball coach that you are, I'm sure you won't be batless for long. Until then, we'll have to rely on my old Smith and Wesson."

"You're armed?"

"It's a requirement. I'm working." He could feel her gaze running along his profile. "I prefer a shoulder holster, but in warm weather like this, it's not practical. If you're not wearing a uniform, people get nervous if they see you packing a gun."

She scooted ahead and looked back at him, then dropped behind him and came up along his other side. The maneuver wrapped Fleur's leash about his waist, and she had to reach around him to untangle him from the dog. She used the opportunity to pat his sides and his waistband.

Daniel reminded himself to breathe.

"Okay," she said, moving to a safe distance once more. "I give. Where is it?"

"Ms. Millbrook, are you asking me to show you my weapon?"

"I am."

"I don't suppose there's any chance of a strip search."

She laughed. A bad sign. He'd obviously put her too much at ease. Her smile did terrible things to his professional detachment.

"None."

"All right." He stopped and hiked up his pants leg.

"That's a gun, all right," Destiny muttered, leaning down for a closer look. Fleur trotted over to investigate, and Destiny tugged her away. "It's smaller than a baseball bat."

"Which makes it easier to carry. And it's got a quicker action, too."

"Hmm. Small and quick. Not exactly the qualities I look for in a . . . weapon."

Laughter exploded from Daniel's chest. He let go of his pants leg and stared at Destiny. She was in the process of turning purple.

Daniel tried out a lecherous grin. "I'll have to start wearing my .45 if I want to make a bigger impression. On the bad guys, of course."

Destiny put a hand over her mouth, trying to hold back her laughter. "Wouldn't a .45 make your socks lumpy?"

She'd just double-dared him, and he couldn't disappoint

her. "I don't need socks to make my gun look bigger."

She choked, her eyes dancing. "I'm glad to hear it, Detective."

"Yes, well, I'm a professional. To work?" He proceeded along the path, biting back his amusement. But he noticed as they turned the next curve that Destiny paused and looked once more over her shoulder at the way they had come.

Just nerves. Understandable nerves. But the memory of the strangely familiar figure he'd glimpsed earlier caused the hair on the nape of his neck to prickle all the same.

Chapter 5

"So much for the 'He has to call. It's his job' theory," Destiny muttered, wrenching a volume of *Books in Print* into place on the shelf behind the library reference desk. "So he cooked you lunch. So he spent all afternoon in the park with you. Apparently he just enjoys his job."

And, just as apparent, an aborted strangling with no leads wasn't high on his list of priority cases. Destiny hadn't heard a word from Daniel Parks since saying good-bye to him in the parking lot of Sequoia Pacific Park on Saturday afternoon.

"And here it is, Monday morning," she derided herself, rolling her chair to her desk.

She wouldn't even be thinking of him, of his intense blue eyes, his perplexed eyebrows, the freedom of his deep laugh, if not for her sister. Serena had called her four times Sunday, afraid to miss any new developments.

"He's adorable," she had raved, ignoring Destiny's attempts to change the subject. "And he's unmarried and can cook. It doesn't get much better than that."

"He's probably got some gorgeous girl who—"

"Baby, he thinks you're about the hottest thing to walk into his life since Jasper County outlawed firecrackers."

Destiny had been glad her sister couldn't see her blush. It would only have encouraged her. "Right, Reenie. That's what you said about Brandon Munsch in high school, and all he wanted were my chemistry notes. Besides, Daniel's not my type. Not at all."

"That's right. He's not a feckless jerk who's going to disappear one afternoon and blame his artistic muse for breaking your heart."

"You know that from having spent all of half an hour in his company."

"I did a tarot reading when I got home." Serena paused, waiting for comment. Destiny honored the statement with the dead silence it deserved. "Daniel showed up as the king of pentacles—wise, successful, reliable—"

"Boring."

"You think Daniel's boring?" Serena had asked, a dare in her voice. "When he looks at you with those drop-dead gorgeous blue eyes full of desperate yearning . . ."

Destiny had hung up, cutting off the conversation, but she had found it more difficult to cut off the train of thought her sister had begun.

Despite Serena's concern that Destiny hadn't so much as been out on a date in over a year—and it had been nearly two since Alain left her—Destiny felt a sense of rightness when she thought about her current life. She enjoyed her job. Not only did she get to read the most recent Tony Hillermans and Janet Evanoviches as soon as they hit the shelves, but she got paid for talking books, for doing research, for listening to the most esoteric interests of a huge variety of people.

She loved her home. Since moving to Hope Point from Sacramento after her sister's divorce last year, she'd wondered how she'd survived living so far from the sea. Early in the morning, before the highway and her neighbors awoke, she could stand on her front stoop and hear the distant roar of the ocean, smell the salt in the air. She loved the redwoods, loved the beach, and had even developed a certain fondness for the fog and the rain—encouraging Serena to threaten to have her carted away to the loony bin.

She loved living near her sister (when her sister wasn't driving her loonier than the rain), loved the opportunity to be part of her niece's life. She'd known how exasperating twelve-year-olds could be before signing up to coach Sarah's summer softball team, but she hadn't known how much fun they were. When they weren't driving her even crazier than Serena could.

In general, her life satisfied her quite well, thank you very much. If she wanted someone to watch TV with in the evening, she had Fleur.

She didn't need a man to start her dreaming of family and forever and then leave her, more alone than she'd been before she met him.

And she certainly didn't need to sit around daydreaming about an anal-retentive cop to whom she ranked somewhere below convenience store break-ins in interest. Even if he did have a dusky tan that showed off the definition of his arm muscles. Even if his sandy hair fell carelessly across his forehead. Even if he had the sexiest sun wrinkles at the corners of his eyes . . .

"Even if he's long gone out of your life," Destiny growled to herself in disgust. "Maybe you could commit another pseudo-homicide. That seemed to capture his attention the first time. Get a life, Millbrook."

"Excuse me?"

She glanced up sharply, plastering on a helpful smile that said, "May I help you? I'm perfectly sane. You're in good hands."

"The woman at the check-out counter said you could help me?" The young man standing in front of her desk appeared more hopeful than doubtful. He obviously hadn't heard her contemplating murder.

He looked like a weekend surfer, his cap on backwards, wearing sandals and faded green shorts, but he'd cut his ruddy hair to conform to workday rules and wore an expensive watch on his wrist. In his early twenties, medium-height, slender, he wouldn't stand out in a crowd, but he had a crooked smile that could charm an angel out of its halo.

"I'll try." Destiny smiled back. "What's your question?"

The young man leaned a little closer, his tone conspiratorial. "I need a recipe for eggplant parmigiana."

"Eggplant parmigiana," she repeated, keying *VEGETARIAN COOKERY* into her terminal. "Is this a secret mission, Mr. Bond?"

He grinned. "You have no idea, Moneypenny."

"A girl," she guessed. Cookbook titles scrolled up her screen.

"She said eggplant parmigiana was her favorite dish." He shrugged. "I told her it was my specialty."

"Cookbooks are in the 640's. I'm pulling up a couple of titles to get you started." Destiny made notes on a piece of scratch paper. "So now you have to make good, eh?"

"She's driving up from San Francisco this afternoon. You don't happen to have a favorite recipe of your own?"

Destiny snorted. "If it doesn't have chocolate in it or it can't be microwaved, don't ask for my advice. Here you go."

He clutched the piece of paper to his chest. "You've saved my life. Or at least my love life."

"Don't thank me until after she's tasted your new specialty."

"The name's Westing, Jake Westing." He held out a hand, which she shook. "I'm forever in your debt, Miss . . . ?"

"Destiny Millbrook." She tapped her nametag.

He blinked. "Oh, right." He leaned away from the desk, about to make another comment, when his posture changed abruptly. He twisted his cap forward over his face and turned his body sideways. His blue eyes widened in clandestine horror.

"My boss," he choked. "I called in sick with the stomach flu."

"You certainly look ill enough," Destiny said, tamping down her smile.

"Which way to the 600's?"

She pointed, and Jake Westing scuttled away into the stacks.

"Slacker."

Destiny looked up into a familiar patrician face. It took her a second to place the man. Daniel's friend Philip. From the park.

"Me?" she asked.

"No." His green eyes traveled past her into the rows of bookshelves. "That young man who was just speaking with you. He resembled someone who's supposed to be sick as a dog at home right now. Do you know his name?"

So Philip was Jake's boss. Well, she'd never make it in MI6 if she couldn't keep a secret. "Sorry. What can I do for you, Mr. . . . ?"

"Philip. Philip Brooks."

For the second time that morning a man with a beautiful smile offered her his hand. She'd have to mention it to Serena—why bother with moonlight when she could meet perfectly nice non-stranglers while basking in the glow from her computer screen?

"Destiny—"

"Destiny Millbrook." He pointed to her nametag. "I guessed." That smile again. "And I don't need any help. I just stopped by to say hello, as I promised. On my way to plow through more dull records. Actually, I'm supposed to meet a client . . . Ah, there she is. Over here, Mrs. Geary."

Destiny knew Pleasance Geary was sixty-five, but she didn't look like anyone's sweet old grandma. At five-eleven, she towered over the dapper man in the pinstripe suit following behind her. She wore a stretch polyester outfit with a bird of paradise splashed across the front and had her gray hair tucked up under a floppy yellow hat, but that didn't soften the iron will in her steel gray eyes.

Nor did it disguise the muscles she'd developed over a lifetime of farm work. Destiny would never forget driving Pleasance's granddaughter, Gemma, home to Hideaway Hill one afternoon to find Pleasance in the orchard pruning her fruit trees with a chain saw.

"Destiny!" Pleasance exclaimed, marching over to her desk. "Gemma says you're starting that Delaney girl at catcher this Saturday."

Destiny scrambled to switch gears into coaching mode. "You know I alternate them, Pleasance. Sarah's pitching Saturday. I want to have Gemma catching when Casey's on the mound next week. She's better at fielding Casey's wild pitches."

The older woman gave a wry smile. "And she's not saying that just to get the old lady off her back, either, Barris. Gemma's the best catcher she's got."

The middle-aged man in the pin-striped suit beside her nodded politely. "I'm a soccer fan, myself, I'm afraid."

The wispy gray hair floating around his rounded head reminded Destiny of the stereotype of the absent-minded professor, but his eyes looked sharp enough as he smiled at her.

"Barris Williams." He offered her his hand.

"Destiny Millbrook."

"What an intriguing name. It fits you."

Destiny thought she heard a hint of the British Isles in his voice, but that might have been the fact that he reminded her of the actor Derek Jacobi.

"I've noticed you here before," he said.

She laughed. "I practically live here."

"I'll have to remember to drop by and visit when I come to the library."

"Just don't offend her," Philip broke in, with a wink at Destiny. "I think she's dating a cop."

Destiny felt herself flush. "Oh, no—"

"I didn't know about that," Pleasance said, with a sharp look at Destiny. "I expect Gemma to keep me up-to-date on all the gossip."

"I'm not—"

"Perhaps we ought to let Miss Millbrook get back to work," Barris Williams suggested, a twinkle in his eye as he rescued her. "We can continue our own meeting in the conference room."

"Barris is the local attorney for Salton Enterprises," Pleasance explained. "He wants to help them buy my land dirt cheap. Philip is going to convince him otherwise, to make sure Gemma's future is taken care of."

"We're here to go over some old county records," Philip said. "We're not making any deals today."

"Not with that awful airplane accident on all our minds," Pleasance agreed. "Wouldn't you know Gage Barclay would be as inconvenient dead as he was alive. No offense, Philip. He was a good man, trying to do what he thought was right. He was just mistaken.

"I'll see you at the game Saturday, Destiny. Come along, gentlemen."

As Pleasance strode off toward the small conference room in the back of the library, Barris Williams in her wake, Philip paused a minute to lean over the desk toward Destiny.

"If I'm not back in an hour, call the SWAT team," he whispered.

"I think you and Pleasance can hold your own against Mr. Williams," Destiny said.

"It's not Williams who scares me." He gave her another wink and followed after his companions.

Destiny shook her head and turned back to her computer screen. Her job was rarely dull.

"Are you wearing a new perfume today?" Maddy Chance, the reference librarian, slipped into the chair next to Destiny's. "Eau de Irresistible or something? Or did your sister have one of her friends brew up a love potion for you?" Maddy cocked one red eyebrow at her. "I don't notice the hunks lining up while *I'm* sitting here."

"Philip Brooks?" The man certainly was hunky, Destiny had to admit. She batted her eyelashes at her flame-haired friend. "It's my new hairstyle." She fluffed her mahogany frizz, which remained undaunted by half a bottle of styling gel and a packet of bobby pins. "You, too, can have the look of a goddess. Just make an appointment at Destiny's House of Heavenly Hair."

"Don't touch my head!" Maddy hastily rolled her chair back. "I'm your boss, and if you even look at my hair funny, I'll fire you like that." She snapped her fingers and rolled to her computer terminal. "By the way, there's another one on the phone."

"Another what?"

"Warm-blooded male. For you. Some guy called earlier asking for the name of the 'lovely young woman at the assistance desk.' When he wouldn't believe I was the woman he wanted, I hung up. But this guy knows your name, so I told him I'd see if you were available. Are you?" Maddy wiggled her eyebrows.

"Depends on who it is," Destiny said. "I told Mel Gibson never to call me at work, but he's so impulsive."

"He didn't give me a name, but his voice is sexy. He spoke like this." Maddy lowered her voice, her mimickry sounding primarily like a case of incipient laryngitis. "I transferred him over from circulation. He's on line one."

Rolling her eyes, Destiny reached for the phone. "Hello. Destiny Millbrook speaking."

"I would have told the woman who answered the phone that this was urgent police business, but I was afraid you'd skip town."

She could almost feel Daniel's voice caressing her skin, leaving a flush she couldn't deny. Serena's influence. She barely knew the man. Hadn't thought about him in at least five minutes.

"I haven't been by my safe deposit box to retrieve my passport yet." Her voice sounded reassuringly normal.

"So you're trapped in Hope Point for a while longer."

"Afraid so."

"I didn't want you to think I'd forgotten your case, but I'm running late today, and I won't have time to talk with you about it until six or six-thirty. Could I drop by then?"

"Of course. I baked chocolate cream cheese brownies last night. I can pay you back for the sandwiches the other day." She turned away from Maddy as her face contorted in agony. *Would you like to come over and see my etchings, Detective?*

"Chocolate cream cheese brownies? I'll have to check regulations and make sure I'm allowed to eat those on duty." He didn't seem to have taken it the wrong way. "Six-thirty?"

Destiny breathed again. "Six-thirty."

"Fine. See you then."

Destiny set down the receiver and unclenched her fingers from their death grip on it. He'd called. To talk over the case. No big deal. Nothing to account for the sudden jump in her pulse.

"Is that a date?" Maddy asked, leaning forward to peer at Destiny's face. "You've got a date."

"No! It's not a date."

"It's about time."

"Maddy, it's not a date!"

"Uh-huh." The phone rang, and Maddy reached for it. "I heard you offer him brownies. Your brownies are more sinful than a bottle of wine on the beach. Hello, Jasper County Library, Hope Point Branch, may I help you?"

Destiny tossed a frown at her friend. She'd explain the situation to her later. Offering brownies to a cop who was trying to catch an attempted-murder suspect did not constitute a date; it was more like a civic duty. And Daniel's visit to her house was no big deal. She was not going to stress out about it. Not even going to think about it.

Not going to think about Daniel's solid presence filling up her living room.

Oh, hell. She was going to have to vacuum.

Daniel slipped Fiona's carefully labeled tape into his tape recorder and glanced at his watch. Five-fifteen. Good. He was officially wasting his own time and not Chief Thomas's. He punched the Play button and leaned back, propping his feet on his desk, eyes closed in concentration.

"You think I make idle threats, Barclay?" The voice rasped. "Think again. Think of your pretty wife. Think of your good name. You could lose it all, opposing progress and jobs. Think long and hard, Mr. Supervisor. I'll be watching you."

Smug jerk. Daniel clicked the recording off without opening his eyes. He'd spoken with a couple of people who'd fit the description that day. He'd called everyone he could think of who might want to change Gage Barclay's vote on the ShopSmart project—Salton Enterprises representatives, lawyers, contractors, developers, county commissioners and the rest of the supervisors. But Daniel felt sure he hadn't yet spoken to this particular jerk.

Not that he could do much if he did match the voice to an actual person. The FAA insisted Barclay's plane crash showed no evidence of foul play. The most Fiona could hope for was to create some negative publicity if the threats were traced to Salton Enterprises.

"You'd think you'd have given up the white knight stuff by now, Parks," he muttered, opening his eyes.

His gaze dropped to his wristband. Five-eighteen.

With a curse, he dropped his feet to the floor. He had a lot of work to plow through. He couldn't afford to waste time counting the minutes until six-thirty.

In fact, he could save himself precious time by not dropping by Destiny Millbrook's house at all. A phone call would more than suffice to catch her up on his investigation. *Sorry, we still haven't caught the guy.* Hang up. Thirty seconds tops.

Much more efficient, much wiser than driving to Destiny's house and sharing a plate of brownies with milk. He could only assume that a woman who licked cream cheese off her fingers would do the same with brownie crumbs. And he couldn't repress his curiosity about how it would feel to kiss away the traces of her milk mustache . . .

He would call her. Then he could finish up the paperwork on the bank robbery he'd foiled earlier that day. A teenager, high on OxyContin, had held up Mario's Café, mistaking its entrance for the branch of Northern Shores Federated on the next block. Daniel's collar had been an accident. Gun still dangling from his hand, the kid had stopped Daniel on the street and asked directions to the bank.

Daniel shuffled the stack of forms on his desk and sighed. More hopeless knight-errant work. He'd drop by the county jail tomorrow and try to put the fear of God into the kid. Maybe arrange a talk with the parents. Statistics didn't give him good odds of changing the young man's course, but the kid had no prior arrests. He'd give it a try.

At least the boy had been on an opiate and not methamphetamines. Tom Yap still had a brace on his wrist from his successful, but painful, attempt to handcuff a hopped up kid after a knife fight on the Square two weeks before.

Still, meth was a problem Daniel had almost gotten used to. It seemed as though every other month the sheriff's department busted a methampthetamine lab in unincorporated Garfield a few miles north of Hope Point. But Jasper County hadn't seen the proliferation of OxyContin abuse that plagued the eastern coast of the United States. Daniel hoped the kid he'd arrested that afternoon wasn't the tip of a troublesome iceberg.

The "poor man's heroin" actually cost more on the illegal market than heroin did. Obtained by prescription for legitimate pain relief for as little as four dollars, the same bottle could fetch upwards of two thousand dollars on the street. Cool and trendy, having the same opioid effects as heroin, oxycodone products were also easy to overdose on. Daniel's robbery suspect had snorted enough that he was lucky he hadn't gone into respiratory failure.

The intercom on Daniel's desk buzzed. He sighed. If he'd wanted big city crime, he would have moved to the Bay Area. He punched at the intercom. "Parks here."

"I've got a four-sixty on the line, Detective." Nancy Dennis sounded apologetic; she didn't usually bother him with burglaries.

"Kermit's here, isn't he? He can take care of it."

"Of course. But the man on the line asked for you. Emergency dispatch switched him over to me when he asked for you by name."

Daniel pressed a finger between his eyebrows, testing for

an incipient headache. "Did he give his name?"

"Lars Holmgren."

That didn't ring any bells.

"He lives out on the Terrace. Elderberry Lane."

Daniel lifted his head. Destiny's street. "What's the address?"

"Fourteen-eighteen, but the break-in is at his neighbor's. She asked him to call you while she watched her house. They think the guy might still be in there."

"Get Riggs," Daniel said, already on his feet. "Tell him to grab a fingerprint kit. And tell Holmgren to get his neighbor the hell away from her house."

This last instruction Nancy didn't need the intercom to hear; he was still talking as he burst out of his office, one arm in his jacket, the other adjusting his shoulder holster. Kermit Riggs met him at the door, joining Daniel's dash for his unmarked car.

Daniel had the Chevy out of the parking lot before Kermit could get his door shut. He took a hard right, up the hill toward Destiny's house. It was her house, he knew it. Who else would stand around, unarmed, waiting for a burglar to climb out her window?

Worse yet, what if she'd followed his advice and bought herself some pepper spray and now thought she could use it to take the perp out? His skin prickled with dread.

They reached the Terrace, a community of modest, older homes nestled into the hill above Hope Point like turtledoves in a cote, unpretentious in their contented domesticity. Hardly an exciting venue for a high-rent burglar. In his mind's eye, Daniel saw the kid he'd arrested that afternoon, eyes blank from drugs, gun dangling carelessly from his fingertips. The cops at the station had laughed at his story, but it had been funny only because the idiot hadn't managed to kill anyone.

He could just see Destiny Millbrook, all of five-three, confronting a desperate drug addict with her baseball bat. Except she'd lost her bat on Friday night. He pressed harder on the gas, taking the turn onto Elderberry Lane with a recklessness that forced Kermit to grab for the dashboard.

And there she was, standing on the sidewalk, her concentration focused on her little white house. She held Fleur's leash in a clenched fist, but the dog remained unconcerned by her mistress's tension, lolling in the grass with her white belly exposed to the sky.

Kermit reached the sidewalk first, but Daniel moved more deliberately, willing his heartbeat—and his temper—back under control. Fleur caught sight of Kermit and heaved herself to her feet, waylaying the young officer by wagging everything behind the tip of her nose. Which left Daniel to deal with Destiny.

"I haven't seen anyone leave," she said, barely sparing him a glance as he approached. "I can't see the backyard fence, but Mr. Holmgren's keeping an eye on that from his kitchen. If the guy heard you drive up, he might panic and run. You'd better hurry."

So much for his damsel in distress. He might have been one of her softball pitchers receiving instructions on the mound. Pitch this batter low and away; she can't resist a lowball.

"Do you have your keys?" Daniel struggled to keep his voice even, professional.

"I locked my doors," she said; defensive. "He must have broken in."

"I'd like not to have to."

"Oh." She had the grace to look chagrined as she passed him her key chain. But it didn't slow her down. "It's this key. You'd better try the bathroom off the hall first. There's a window without a screen—"

He interrupted brusquely. "Which one is the back door key? Kerry, you take the rear. I'll give you ninety seconds."

Kermit disentangled himself from the Lab without losing his footing, took the key Daniel offered, and padded across the lawn to the backyard gate.

"Which is Holmgren's house?" Daniel asked.

She pointed to the sky-blue California bungalow on the left. "He was having coffee in his kitchen when—"

"Get in the house with him, and stay there until I come for you." He didn't wait for an argument. "Just do it."

He moved toward the front door without looking back, wondering if he should have given Kermit an extra two minutes so he'd have time to drag Destiny to safety—by her shirt collar if necessary. But as he pulled his gun from its holster, he heard the jingle of Fleur's collar and Destiny's footsteps moving away. He breathed a little easier.

Body pressed to the wall, gun in hand, he unlocked the front door and clicked the doorknob loose from the jamb. He steadied his breath, straining to hear any telltale noises from inside.

His training and his experience had prepared him to expect almost anything he might face on the other side of the door. Destiny's belongings strewn across her rug, broken glass, missing television set. A scared kid hiding in a closet or a desperate thug with a knife or a gun. The dangerous unknown did not become easier to face no matter how many times he had done it, but he was prepared.

He glanced at his watch. Time. He kicked the door, sending it slamming open against the inside wall. He followed, dodging low, his gun ready.

It didn't do him a bit of good.

Destiny pressed up against Mr. Holmgren's kitchen

counter, angling her head for a better view. From here she could see portions of both the front and backyards of her house but not the doors. Kermit and Daniel must be inside by this time.

"He can't have taken the television set," Mr. Holmgren reassured her from his post at his end of the counter, looking out at the low redwood fence that separated their backyards. "If he'd carried that out, I'd've seen it for sure. Did you have anything small he might've pocketed? You should keep your jewelry in a safety deposit box, you know. These days that's about the only safe place on earth. Soon we'll all be living in bank vaults. Would you like something to drink? Coffee?"

"No, thank you."

"It isn't often young people visit, but I might have a soda in the fridge." He started to rise.

"No, really, I'm fine." She smiled gratefully at the old man, and he settled back onto his stool. She figured it was only a matter of time before he remembered the tea tucked away in the back of his cupboard or the lemonade mix in his freezer. The world could end, and Lars Holmgren would be offering God's angels a glass of club soda to take the edge off Armageddon's heat.

"I've lived in this house ten years," Mr. Holmgren said. "Never had a burglary on this block. Not one. The world is changing."

The view from the window remained still, static. Not so much as a flicker of a curtain betrayed life in her house. It must have been ten minutes since Daniel and Kermit had arrived. What could be taking them so long? She could dust every surface in her house in that amount of time; it wasn't that big.

She squelched the voice in her head asking when she'd last dusted *any* surface in her house. Maybe Daniel and Kermit wouldn't notice.

She heard Fleur's foot hit Mr. Holmgren's back door.

"No. You can't go out."

A whine so high as to be almost inaudible pierced her ears.

"She just wants to get that guy who broke into her house."
Mr. Holmgren teetered on his stool as he reached out to pat
the dog's head. Fleur thumped the door again, looking
hopeful.

Destiny frowned at her. "No, she just hates linoleum. She
only tolerates my kitchen because she gets fed there. Fleur,
settle down."

Her house remained quiet. Destiny refused to worry.
Daniel knew what he was doing. He wouldn't get hurt.

"They know what they're doing." Mr. Holmgren's reedy
voice echoed her thoughts. "They do this every day, the police."

That thought failed to comfort her. Every day Daniel
might face deadly situations as a matter of course. It had
never occurred to her how dangerous a policeman's job could
be, even in a small town. It might not have occurred to her
now if it weren't Daniel out there, searching her house for a
desperate burglar, risking his life for her stupid TV.

A crashing sound, faint but distinct in the hush of early
evening, came through the window. From the direction of her
house. From the sound of it, from *inside* her house.

"Did you hear that?"

Mr. Holmgren tottered on his stool again. "Hear what?"

But Fleur had heard. Her ears pricked, and the fur at her
withers began to rise. The hairs on Destiny's neck prickled,
too.

"Something in my house—"

Another crash, louder this time. And a shout. Daniel?
Fleur's hysterical barking drowned any further noise from
outside.

Sudden, aching fear tightened Destiny's throat. "Fleur, hush. Hush!" But the tension in her voice only upset the dog more.

Destiny twisted her neck, seeking a glimpse of her front door, but a juniper bush hid it from view. Instinct screamed for her to act. But if she ran outside now, she would only put herself in danger and possibly jeopardize Daniel's safety.

Unless he'd already fallen victim to the burglar's attack. Even now he could be bleeding to death on her kitchen floor.

She grabbed Fleur's leash. "Call the police station for backup."

Mr. Holmgren caught himself on the counter as he slipped off his stool. "What? Where are you going?"

"To find out what's happening over there."

Fleur strained on the leash, eager to investigate. Destiny followed her out into the living room toward the front door.

"Wait!" Mr. Holmgren hurried after them. "Wait, now. I can't let you do that. You must wait here for the police."

"I've got Fleur with me."

Holmgren looked doubtfully at the dog, who was whining at the delay. "That offers me little comfort, somehow."

"That's because you know what a pussycat she is. But a stranger won't. I'm going."

"No. He might be out there. He might have a weapon."

She reached for the doorknob. He reached for the leash.

A sharp knock at the door froze them both.

Chapter 6

"Who is it, please?" The question came in an old man's voice, quavering with tension.

"Detective Daniel Parks."

"Daniel!" He heard the relief in Destiny's cry as she wrenched open the door. For a crazy second he thought she might fling herself into his arms, but she stopped in the doorway. Fleur did not. The excited Lab yanked Destiny off her feet, forcing Daniel to grab her to prevent her from sprawling into Mr. Holmgren's impatiens.

"Fleur!" New fear filled Destiny's voice as the dog dashed for her house, trailing the leash behind her.

"It's all right. Kerry will catch her."

"But the burglar—"

"No one's there."

He was practically murmuring in her ear and was acutely aware that she was clinging to his shoulders, that his hands rested against her ribs to steady her. Daniel felt anything but steady himself, his nerves reacting to the warmth of her side along his chest, her thigh pressed against his.

She smelled good. It had been a long time since he'd been close enough to a woman to smell her hair. A long time since he'd felt a woman's body against his. And despite the urgency of the current situation, his body liked it. He liked it. Liked having Destiny cling to him for just a moment . . .

"Are you all right?" He wondered if he imagined the flush in her cheeks as she found her feet and stepped away.

"I'm fine. Are you? We heard a crash."

"That was . . . an accident." The reminder of the tense,

unsettling search through her house effectively returned his mind to active duty. "You'll need to see if anything's missing, but we didn't find any signs of an intruder."

She took that in. "He broke in and didn't steal anything?"

"You drove up not long after I saw him go through your gate." An old man Daniel assumed to be Lars Holmgren stepped out onto the porch. Brilliant white hair framed his face, cheeks ruddy from a life spent outdoors. Watery blue eyes peered at Daniel. "Perhaps that frightened him away."

"There's no evidence of a break-in at all."

"He didn't get inside?" He could hear the relief in Destiny's voice. He'd felt it, too, once his adrenaline level had recovered from the expectation of finding a lunatic behind every door in her house. The idea of a stranger violating the safety of her home made his stomach churn. If Holmgren hadn't noticed the guy, and she'd walked in on an intruder . . .

"That's what we want you to confirm. The back door was locked, but the kitchen window was open a crack. You didn't actually see the intruder break in, Mr. Holmgren?"

The old man shook his head. "I saw this man sneaking through Miss Millbrook's back gate. He could be a friend of hers, I'm thinking, I don't know. But I don't like his look. So I wait for her to come home and ask her if she's expecting a visitor. Then I call the police."

"And you said it wasn't long after you saw the man that Ms. Millbrook returned?"

"No. I was still trying to decide what to do." He let out a worried puff of breath. "I don't want to be a busybody. But Miss Millbrook is all alone over there, so I try to watch out for her."

Daniel wondered if the old man owned a baseball bat.

"Thank you," Destiny said, giving Holmgren a quick hug. "It's nice to know you're right next door."

Holmgren's cheeks reddened even more. "If neighbors watched out for each other, we wouldn't have to live in safety deposit boxes."

Destiny started toward her house, and Daniel fell in behind her with Holmgren.

"Do you think you'd recognize the man if you saw him again?"

Holmgren's face wrinkled in doubt. "My eyes are still okay, Detective. Better than my ears, you know. But I didn't get a good look at him. A young man, maybe. He looked athletic. I don't think he's any taller than you are. I thought he seemed suspicious because he wore a knit cap in this good weather."

"A ski mask?"

"No, no. Just a cap. Like a seaman wears."

A sudden image of a young Lars Holmgren, his Scandinavian cheekbones reddened by a salty wind as he hauled fish into a creaking boat flashed through Daniel's mind. The old man placed a gnarled hand on Daniel's shoulder, his grip strong, and Daniel thought that young sailor wasn't as faded away as he looked at first glance.

"She said to ask for you, Detective, that she had a friend in the police department." Holmgren's pale blue eyes held his, and Daniel could believe they were as sharp as his own. "I can't explain it, but I thought this man knew where he was going, that he was not picking her house at random. I don't want to frighten Miss Millbrook, but I will tell you. Keep an eye out for her. I don't want her to be hurt."

"I understand," Daniel assured him. "We'll catch this guy if he keeps hanging around your neighborhood, don't worry. You call right away if you see anything else suspicious."

Holmgren nodded, satisfied, and squeezed Daniel's shoulder once more before turning back to his house. He didn't seem to realize how little Daniel had been able to promise.

He'd already put an excessive amount of his time, and Kermit's, into investigating a break-in that hadn't happened. And he'd waste more time having the prints Kermit had lifted from her door and windowsill checked against her prints and her sister's and his own to see if they came up with any extras. Such as the refrigerator repairman's or the landlord's. Pointless. But he'd do it anyway. Because he didn't want her hurt any more than Lars Holmgren did.

He entered Destiny's open front door. Kermit had righted the end table and lamp he'd tripped over and had apparently found a hand-held vacuum with which to clean up the bits of broken light bulb that had littered the rug.

Daniel heard voices and found Destiny and Kermit inside the doorway to her bedroom.

"I don't know," Destiny was saying, her voice tight with stress. "Nothing seems to be missing. Nothing valuable." She gestured to the iMac computer and the laser printer on her desk, then to the mother-of-pearl box on the top of her chest of drawers. "My good jewelry is all in there. Nothing's gone."

She glanced at Daniel, her eyes troubled. "But I think he's been in here."

"Why?"

She shrugged and shook her head. "It's more of a feeling. . . ." She moved to the desk, pulled open a drawer. Daniel glimpsed pens, paper clips, postcards, old bills—the sort of melange he'd have expected to find in Destiny's desk drawers. "This doesn't look the way I left it."

She saw the expressions on his and Kermit's faces. "I know, I know. But it doesn't. And my closet. And my bed."

She brushed a hand over her bedspread, a comforter in a soft gray and lilac floral pattern. Daniel hadn't noticed it earlier, intent on checking beneath the bed and in the closet for intruders. But now he observed how the turned-down spread revealed the rumpled pink sheets beneath. She must have pushed aside the covers that morning, warm with sleep, slipping her bare feet out from under the sheets . . . He shook the image from his mind.

She tugged the comforter in a futile attempt to neaten it. "It's like someone pushed things aside or picked things up and tried to put them back as they were but didn't quite get it right."

"That might have been us," Daniel reminded her. "I pushed stuff around in your closet during my search."

"How about the shower curtain?" She walked back down the hall to the bathroom.

Kermit followed her and leaned his long body around the edge of the doorframe. "Daniel checked the shower."

"I pulled the curtain aside and put it back again."

"It was closed when you came in? You're sure?" Destiny asked, tugging the blue plastic aside.

"I'm sure." One didn't forget pulling aside a shower curtain if a dangerous criminal might lurk behind it.

"That's what I mean. I'm sure I left it open after my shower this morning."

Kermit reached around her to pull it closed again. "You really should leave it stretched like this, you know. If you let it sit crumpled open when it's wet, it'll mildew. . . ." His voice trailed off as his fair complexion reddened. "Fleur's in the backyard. I'll check on her."

He scooted past Daniel and down the hall.

Destiny raised an eyebrow. "Are all cops obsessive-compulsive?"

Daniel couldn't suppress a smile. She did that to him at the most inappropriate times: sneaked in under his defenses.

And he liked it. He wanted to stick around and find out what turn her mind would take next. Dangerous.

"It doesn't hurt to have an eye for detail in this job."

She ran a hand through her tortured hair, blowing out a sigh. "All right. What do I do now?"

She must really be shaken, if she was asking for advice. "Come back to the kitchen and sit down. A cup of tea wouldn't do you any harm."

She followed him down the hall. "What about the shower curtain?"

"You want my opinion?"

"You're the cop."

In other words, no. He gave it to her anyway. "Everything in your home is bound to look strange to you after an incident like this. Just the idea of a break-in disrupts your feeling of security, changes how your house appears to you. I'm not surprised you think things seem a little off."

"You think I'm being paranoid?" she asked. She looked more unsettled than defiant.

He flicked on the burner beneath her teakettle. "I think you ought to keep your eyes and ears open, and if you find anything missing or even feel something's wrong, you call me immediately. Okay?"

She almost smiled. "Okay. Thank you."

He found a mug drying in the drainer and dropped in a bag of mint tea from a box on the microwave. "That's what I'm here for."

She leaned against the counter. "I doubt making tea is in your job description."

"Learned it at the academy," he said. "Right between loading a pistol and writing parking tickets."

She did smile, and he decided he liked the skeptical tilt of her eyes.

92

"I mean it, though," she continued. "After Friday night, dragging you out to find a body that wasn't there, and then today—the burglary that never happened. You could have written me off as a fruitcake."

The teapot whistled, and he poured the water. "I happen to be fond of fruitcake."

It was a stupid comment meant to make her smile again. But when her fingers touched his as he handed her the mug of tea, something twisted in the words. And he knew he shouldn't catch her gaze at that moment, but he did anyway, and he couldn't let go of the mug, and he couldn't smile it away. And he wasn't a cop, and she wasn't a crime victim; she was a beautiful woman with eyes that widened and darkened, and he wanted to brush her lips with his thumb . . .

The screen door crashed as the back door flew open in a tangle of yellow Lab and gangly cop. Daniel's fingers slipped from the mug and so did Destiny's. Mint tea and pottery exploded on the kitchen floor.

For a second silence reigned. And then Kermit moaned. "Please tell me that wasn't my fault."

"She's beautiful, just beautiful. Really a good-looking girl."

Daniel grunted, checking both ways and flicking on his signal before turning left. It was a poor attempt to atone for his wild driving earlier. No sense in angering the traffic gods.

"And sweet as anything," Kermit continued, gushing in a way Daniel thought out of character for him. "Don't you think?"

" 'Sweet' isn't the word I'd have used," Daniel muttered. Touchy, independent, untidy, *sexy* . . . but sweet?

Kermit laughed. "Grouch. Don't pretend you don't like her."

Was he that obvious? "I didn't say that."

If his tone said "change the subject," Kermit didn't notice. "A charmer, that's what she is. Too bad she's taken."

Taken? Even Holmgren had mentioned that she lived on her own. Daniel turned the car into the police station parking lot.

"I guess it wouldn't look good on my record if I kidnapped her," Kermit mused. "But now I know what I want. I'm going to find myself one just like her. I wonder if she's gun-shy?"

Daniel choked, hitting the brake with enough force to throw Kermit against his seat belt. "Fleur! You're talking about the dog!"

Kermit stared at him. "Yeah, Fleur. Who did you think I . . ."

Daniel noticed with impressive detachment that Kermit's fair skin turned pink all the way to the roots of his fair hair when he tried not to laugh. The freckles on his nose stood out.

"Not that—" Kermit caught his breath. "Not that Ms. Millbrook isn't lovely, too, but I doubt she'd have much interest in retrieving ducks." The laughter broke free, and he almost struck his head on the dash.

"Careful, you'll hurt yourself." Daniel climbed out of the car and slammed his door.

Kermit followed, tripping over the parking bumper. "I'm sorry."

Daniel resisted the temptation to slam the station door in his subordinate's face. "Just drop it." He waved at Nancy and turned into his office.

"I'm sorry," Kermit repeated, following him. "It wasn't *that* funny."

Daniel dropped into his chair. "Okay, okay. Now—"

"It was just the look on your face . . ." Kermit struggled

heroically to regain control. "You do like her, don't you?"

"Fleur?"

"No. Destiny Millbrook."

"She seems like a good person." Daniel ruffled through the pile of papers on his desk. "It's nice to run into one of those now and then."

Kermit folded his long frame into one of the metal chairs opposite Daniel. "That's not what I meant."

Daniel glared at him over the papers. "Don't you have something you should be doing?"

"I'm taking my break."

"Take it elsewhere." Daniel opened his desk drawer and pulled out a paper clip. He imagined Destiny would find it obsessive-compulsive to have a plastic organizer in his desk for different sized paper clips. He doubted Destiny could even find a paper clip in her desk drawer. She probably had to buy a new box every time she wanted one.

Scratch that. She probably never used paper clips.

"Well?"

"What?" He glared at Kermit again.

"What are you going to do about it?"

The young man either had more nerve or fewer brain cells than Daniel had given him credit for.

"Nothing."

"You ought to ask her out."

"This is a case, Kerry."

"She'd say yes."

"That's immaterial. I'm not going to ask her out."

"When was the last time you went out on a date? Have you dated anyone since your divorce?"

Daniel dropped the clipped papers into his to-do-later-when-I-absolutely-have-to box. "Riggs, I don't know if you've noticed, but I outrank you, and my social life is none of your business."

"Sorry." Kermit unfolded himself from the chair. "I just thought you might want to talk about it. You're the one who told me that being human isn't a bad trait in a cop."

Daniel remembered the Kermit Riggs who had joined the force a year and a half ago—younger, ganglier, unsure of himself. Back when Daniel's divorce was still dragging through the spring like a late thaw. Taking the rookie officer under his wing had forced his mind off his own troubles. Through Kermit he had found his energy again. Of course, Edgar had helped, too, and Edgar never interfered in his personal life.

"It's all right, Kerry. I know you mean well. But I keep my work and my private life separate. That's one lesson the divorce taught me. Now go find some work to do, or I'll tell Lieutenant Marcy you've got too much time on your hands."

"Okay. I'm going. But Destiny Millbrook is nothing like Tessa—nothing against the ex-Mrs. Parks, of course. If you don't ask her out, you're crazy. Sir."

Daniel swallowed his caustic reply in order to catch the pencil holder Kermit knocked off the desk in his hasty retreat. He settled for a killing glare at Kermit's back as the young officer escaped out the office door.

He'd only be crazy if he *did* ask Destiny Millbrook out. That's certainly how she made him feel. Crazy.

Of course cops were human. Despite the depravity and callousness and petty meanness he dealt with almost every day, he still thought being human was something worth being. But he was also a professional. If he didn't focus on his job, someone could get hurt. As long as Destiny's case remained open, it was part of his job.

Not to mention that whatever his instincts said—and Destiny's presence wreaked havoc on his instincts—there was still the possibility that she knew more about these strange crimes against her than she was letting on, that she was not the innocent victim she portrayed. He had plenty of good reasons for not pursuing his attraction to her.

It had nothing to do with his breakup with Tessa. Nothing to do with a fear of being hurt again, whatever Kermit might think.

He peeled the sticky note with Destiny's phone number on it off his desktop and crumpled it. The number was typed in her file. He'd only call her if the case broke open, which at this point seemed unlikely.

If the idea of never seeing her again disturbed him, he'd recover soon enough. He'd even forget that he'd never had the chance to taste her brownies.

He tossed the crumpled note into the trash.

It wasn't the brownies he'd miss. The thought struck him as he turned his gaze back to his paperwork. It wasn't the scent of her hair or even her skeptical smile. It was the way he felt when he was with her. As though a sunny day were a precious gift, a walk in the park a blessing from heaven. She made him feel human again, in the best sense of the word.

He felt as if he'd thrown away a great deal more than a telephone number.

The phone rang Wednesday morning as Destiny finished pouring milk over her cereal.

"Of course." Soggy corn flakes—a great start to a gray day. "Destiny?"

She didn't recognize the ragged voice. Not Daniel. She cursed herself for the thought. She hadn't heard from Daniel since the non-break-in Monday. She hadn't really expected a lead to develop in either of her cases, but he might at least have kept her informed. "Hello?"

"Is this Destiny Millbrook?"

Sudden nerves prickled down her back. Not Serena. Not Maddy. Who on earth would call her at seven-thirty on a Wednesday morning?

"Who is this?" she demanded.

"Destiny? It's Pleasance Geary."

Destiny dropped her forehead into her free hand and took a deep breath. Maybe she was in danger of becoming paranoid, after all.

"Sorry, Pleasance, I didn't recognize your voice. How can I help you?"

"It's the Jasper crud," the older woman growled, giving her complaint the local name for any miserable, dripping cold. "Me and Gemma's both got it. I wanted to let you know she won't be at practice this afternoon. Probably not tomorrow, either."

Destiny bit back a sigh. Summer colds were the worst. This one would probably make the rounds through her whole team. She could only hope all the girls would be well enough to play in the tournament.

"Thanks for letting me know, Pleasance. I'll hope she'll feel up to playing on Saturday."

"Me, too. We're both grouches when we're sick."

"You two take care of yourselves."

"Nothing a little chicken soup won't cure. Wait, Destiny?"

"Yes?"

"You're working today, right? I didn't wake you up? I just wanted to catch you before you left."

Destiny smiled at the woman's belated concern. Pleasance Geary was tough as nails, but Destiny had grown fond of her over the course of the summer. "I'm up. I'll be heading out the door in a few minutes. You caught me at the perfect time."

"Good. I'll talk to you later."

Destiny set the receiver down and turned back to her cereal. It sagged on her spoon. Her life had definitely returned to normal. She had to stop expecting every phone call to be a new emergency. She had to stop expecting every phone call to be from Daniel.

She dumped the mushy cereal down the garbage disposal and fought open the box of corn flakes. Just as she reached for the milk, the phone rang again.

"Great." Probably her short stop come down with chicken pox.

"May I speak with Destiny Millbrook, please?"

The male voice at the other end of the line sounded vaguely familiar, and his brisk efficiency made her feel even more cross by comparison.

"Yes, this is Destiny Millbrook. Who's this?"

"Sergeant Fleming at the police department, ma'am. I've just had a call from Detective Parks. I understand you were attacked in the park the other night and managed to injure your assailant."

"Yes."

"Well, ma'am, a body's washed ashore at Union Cove."

"A *body?*"

"Yes, ma'am. Wearing a hooded gray sweatshirt. The corpse also has a head wound consistent with being struck by a blunt object. Detective Parks thinks it may be the man who attacked you. He wondered if you'd mind making an identification."

"I—I don't . . ." Destiny put a hand on the counter as the room darkened briefly. The man who attacked her. Dead. She didn't know how to feel about that. She hadn't been wishing for *that* kind of excitement. "I didn't get a good look at the man. I don't think I'd be much help."

"I understand, ma'am, but it's procedure. It shouldn't take more than a few minutes once you get to the cove. Do you need directions?"

Dead. How? If the blow from her baseball bat had killed him, how had he ended up in the ocean? Would she have to go to court to defend herself against manslaughter charges?

"Ma'am? You take the highway up the coast—"

"Yes, I know how to get to Union Cove." Fleur loved the beach there. "It will take me about fifteen or twenty minutes."

"That's fine, ma'am. I'll inform Detective Parks."

She hung up and dropped the corn flake box on the counter. So much for her appetite. She sent Fleur out back for her morning constitutional and called Maddy to let her know she'd be late for work.

When Fleur saw that Destiny had changed into jeans instead of slacks, the dog ran to grab her leash from its hook by the front door, thinking the weekend had miraculously returned.

"Sorry, girl. You're staying here. I'm going to the beach, but it won't be fun."

Fleur didn't believe her, and Destiny could hear the dog crying as she made her way down the walk to her car.

Fog had rolled in overnight, turning late summer into early fall. Destiny knew that even the heaviest fog could lift by noon, the weather playing a mischievous game of "Gotcha!" so the sunshine would be even more appreciated. But this morning she felt as though the fog could last clear through winter. It chilled her and caused her temperamental car door lock to stick.

A body. As she backed the car into the street, Sergeant Fleming's phone call replayed in her mind. Why would Daniel make her drive all the way out to Union Cove, especially when he knew she hadn't taken a close look at her attacker? Surely the police normally called people into the morgue for identifications.

A burst of anger displaced the cold distress that had settled in her stomach when she first heard the news. Just her luck to be stuck with a detective so obsessive about his cases that he didn't give any thought to the victim's feelings.

As she reached the highway, though, her anger eased. Driving up the coast when she should be at work, watching the breakers lift spray from black rocks far below, gave her the same heady sense of guilty freedom as playing hooky from school once had.

If not for the knowledge that she was going to identify—or rather, be unable to identify—a dead body, she'd be glad for the chance to escape from town for a few hours.

Perhaps Daniel had been thinking of that when he'd spoken with Sergeant Fleming. Perhaps he had wanted to spare her the ordeal of entering the morgue. Perhaps he had been glad of the excuse to see her again.

Destiny snorted. She was as bad as Serena. More likely, the appearance of the body had re-ignited his suspicion that she had concocted the whole attack on Friday night in order to get rid of a troublesome boyfriend—not that she hadn't considered something of the sort with what's-his-name—and he wanted to watch her reaction when faced with her wicked deed.

She'd brave his challenge, do her civic duty, and then she would drive to work and try to put the whole business behind her.

Still, she was glad she'd had time to shower and tame her hair before the call came in. She'd worn her one pair of tight jeans—after all, they were the only pair not in the wash. And an emerald cotton shirt that accented the red highlights in her hair—because it had long sleeves. But it wouldn't hurt her feelings if Daniel noticed that she looked good this morning.

She reminded herself again of the body, squelching her thoughts of Daniel, and took stock of where she was on the road. To her right, Sitka spruce and red alders marched up the hills into the gray damp, the green of the trees shimmering in bright contrast to the fog. To the left, the cliff fell away to the sea, only the whitecaps distinguishing the gray water from the gray sky.

The parking lot for Union Cove was only another mile ahead. She took a deep breath to steady herself . . .

And felt the steering wheel twist violently in her grasp, heard a sound that she knew must be a tire blowing. And a sound like a giant firecracker echoing down the cliffs. A gunshot.

The road curved ahead of her, and her thoughts about the body, the tire, and even the gunshot faded away as she realized her Rabbit was skidding across the center line of the highway, directly into the path of an oncoming car.

Chapter 7

If she'd been driving any faster, she'd be dead. That was Destiny's first thought as her VW shuddered and died against the guardrail. The bronze Chevy had swerved past her as her Rabbit had spun 180 degrees, slamming into the railing to leave her facing the way she'd come. By some miracle, the low metal barrier had held, preventing her from plunging a hundred and fifty feet to the rocks below.

Her second thought was that someone had shot out her tire. Her third, that that particular someone might be pissed that he hadn't taken her out with the first bullet.

She couldn't get out the driver's side door; she'd be exposed. But she thought the Rabbit had bounced back enough from the railing that she could slide out the passenger door, giving her room to crouch with the car between her and the opposite side of the road.

As she tried to crawl over the gearshift, she suddenly realized why vanity was considered one of the deadly sins. Tight jeans were not designed for escaping car wrecks. She scrambled over the stick shift and fumbled with the door handle. Despite some crumpling from the impact, the door opened far enough for her to squeeze out.

As she huddled against the side of the Rabbit, gulping for air, the rumble of a car engine drowned out the roaring in her ears. Tires ground into the gravel along the edge of the road behind her. Panic spun her around against the low guardrail, as she desperately sought an escape route. She took her first look over the cliff and wished she hadn't. Nothing broke the sheer drop to the waves below, unless you counted the rocks that the waves were slamming against.

The old, growling car pulled up behind hers, and Destiny recognized the grille. The bronze Chevy she'd almost flattened had returned. The driver was probably a little peeved, but at least he or she wasn't likely to be carrying a high-powered rifle.

In fact, it wasn't just the grille—the whole car looked familiar, and the man climbing out was even more so.

"Daniel!"

He spotted her, and she could actually see the blood drain from his face.

"Destiny! Don't move." He dropped down to squeeze into the space beside her. "What happened? Were you thrown from the car?"

"No, I'm not hurt." But she couldn't say any more, because, in the rush of relief, she began to shake. She grabbed for Daniel's jacket as he neared, needing to touch something besides cold, dead metal. He pulled her close, his hands warm against her back.

She pressed her face against his chest, trying to control her shuddering, moisture from her eyes damp against his shirt. He stroked her hair.

"You gave me quite a scare." His voice against the top of her head sounded as unsteady as she felt. Even through her fear it warmed her. "Are you sure you're not hurt?"

She nodded, not trusting her voice.

She felt him shift to look over the railing. His arms tightened involuntarily. "Next time you decide to have a blowout, could you do it somewhere without a view? Let's see if we can move a little farther away from a sudden swim."

He gripped her arms, preparing to rise, and panic shot through her once more.

"No!" She tugged down on his jacket. "Don't stand up. It

wasn't an accident. Someone shot out my tire."

The lines around Daniel's mouth softened. "I'm sure it sounded that way. I had a tire blow out on the way home from firing practice one afternoon, and I thought my pistol had gone off in the trunk."

"I heard the tire blow," Destiny said. "And I also heard a rifle shot. Two separate sounds."

"Destiny, the echoes around here—"

"It was not an echo. He might still be out there waiting for me."

"Look at me." Daniel brushed the hair back from her cheek. "You've been under a lot of stress this past week."

"You think I'm paranoid."

He made a heroic effort not to smile. "Not paranoid. Stressed. There's a difference. Now, I'm going to go take a look at your tire. I think it's the rear left."

He stood before she could stop him and moved around the back of the car. She tried to swallow her fear. However annoying he could be, she didn't want him killed.

But maybe he was right. Look at how ready she'd been to think someone had entered her home. Maybe the sound *had* been an echo. . . .

A hole spiderwebbed the windshield of Daniel's car a half-second before the sound of the shot cracked against her eardrums. Before she could think to scream, Daniel dove back behind her car, landing sprawled in front of her.

"I think," he said, his eyes wide, "that on further consideration, I believe someone may have shot out your tire."

Destiny might have felt smug if she hadn't been focused on keeping her heart from pounding through her rib cage. "Another—" She took a breath. "—fine deduction, Holmes."

"Thank you, Watson." He pulled himself up into a sitting position, taking care to keep his head low, before sticking a hand inside his jacket to pull out his pistol.

Blood buzzed in her ears. "Can you reach him from here?"

"Not a chance." He dumped the cartridges out of the chamber of the gun and dropped them into his pocket. She could see his deep breathing, but his voice remained calm. "With that rifle, he's got us pinned here. Damn." He scrambled to grab a stray cartridge. "On the plus side, thanks to our position on this cliff, I don't think he can get a clean shot at us unless he shows himself. I'm going to call for some help, and we'll be fine. Don't worry."

Destiny allowed herself a moment of relief, until she looked toward his car. "But you're too close to the guardrail. You can't get in through your passenger door."

"That's what the gun's for."

He stepped over the crash bumper onto the minuscule shoulder between it and the drop to the ocean.

"Daniel!"

"Stay here." He scurried across the short gap between their cars, ducking down beside his passenger door. With one hand on the door handle to steady himself against the impact, he cracked the butt of his gun sharply against the door's window. Two more quick blows and he had the glass mostly cleared.

Destiny's ears cracked again, and she saw another hole in Daniel's windshield.

"You can't go in there!" she shouted. "He'll kill you."

Daniel reloaded his gun. "He's hitting the windshield high. He must have an obstructed view. I just need to grab the handset. If I stay low, I'll be fine."

He set his gun down beside the front tire and shrugged out of his coat. Just as Destiny realized that he was leaving the gun there for her, in case he was wrong about the sniper, he plunged the upper half of his body through the broken window.

Destiny thought she might be screaming, but the explosion of rifle fire echoing around her drowned her voice. She swung her leg over the metal barrier, sending a spray of gravel plunging downward. But even as she reached Daniel's car, he'd pulled back out, clutching his radio handset.

"Code thirty. Officer under fire. Request assistance."

Destiny grabbed his free hand, and he squeezed it tightly.

"I thought I told you to stay by your car. No, Nancy, not you. I'm on 101, half a mile north of the Bridge Creek cutoff. A sniper with a rifle."

His sandy hair ruffled around his face in uncharacteristic disarray, and blood oozed from a scratch over his right eye. But his voice remained steady, in control, as he spoke to the dispatcher. Only the pressure on her hand betrayed his inner tension.

"Yes, call in the highway patrol. And we'll need a tracking unit . . ."

She sank beside him on the cold gravel, tuning out the words, the simple sound of his voice her link to reality. She watched her feet dangling over the cliff edge and smelled the fishy salt spray rising from the waves below, and she wasn't afraid. Because Daniel's hand still held hers, and it was warm and alive, and for now they were safe.

Daniel paused in the doorway to his office. Destiny sat hunched in one of the metal chairs he'd bought at a school discard sale, her hands tight around the cup of reheated coffee he'd poured for her. Once more he felt the fierce, protective urge to take her in his arms, to hold her until she forgot her recent terror.

Instead, he crossed to his side of the desk. She looked up, and though he saw traces of fear in the tightness around her mouth, he also saw that she hadn't withdrawn into it as he'd feared. Life burned deep and strong in those warm brown eyes, and he felt another fierce emotion, which he buried before he could acknowledge it.

"Did they catch him?"

Daniel shook his head. "He had a vehicle on Bridge Creek Road. The CHP has set up a roadblock inland, but there's a strong possibility he'll slip by on one of those dirt access roads."

He didn't want to frighten her, but her eyes demanded the truth. And he was going to need the truth from her.

"I know you'll do all you can." She took a sip of coffee. He knew she was still in shock because it didn't make her grimace. "Daniel, I . . . You saved my life."

For some reason her gratitude disturbed him. "That's my job."

She had the nerve to smile. "Thank goodness you were on duty, then."

That's what was bothering him. He didn't want the warmth in her voice to be for his job or because he might have saved her life. He wanted that warmth for himself.

He'd had bullets fly past him once before in his life, and the fear he'd felt then had been nothing compared to the terror he'd experienced today, knowing the sniper wanted Destiny dead. He hadn't faced down the danger because it was his job. He'd done it because he couldn't let her be killed.

Destiny's smile faded. "But I don't understand what you were doing there."

"I live up in Shell Creek. I was on my way to work."

Her Styrofoam cup paused on the way to her lips. "But what about the body?"

He hoped he hadn't missed something crucial. Being shot at was disturbing, but he was sure he would have noticed a corpse. "What body?"

"At Union Cove."

He shook his head. "Sorry. I didn't listen to the news this morning. Did someone find a body on the beach up there?"

"I got a call this morning." She scooted forward on her chair, resting her cup on his desk. "From Sergeant Fleming, telling me—"

"Fleming? You mean Fisher?"

"No, I'm sure he said Fleming. . . . You don't have a Sergeant Fleming in the department?"

The way she said it made his spine prickle. "No."

Her eyelids fluttered closed, and he couldn't stop himself from reaching for her hand. Her fingers felt limp and nerveless. He rubbed them with his thumb. "Tell me what he said."

She opened her eyes. "He told me you'd found a body at Union Cove, a young man in a hooded sweatshirt with a head wound. He said you wanted me to come identify the body."

"If we want an ID, we have people come to the morgue." But she'd figured that out for herself now.

"I thought it was odd, at the time, but I thought maybe you . . . He set me up. To kill me."

Her agonized disbelief wrenched his heart. Nobody could possibly have a reason to kill her. Yet nobody went to all that trouble for nothing.

"Destiny, why would someone want you dead?"

Her gaze met his as she pulled her hand free. She was no fool. She knew what he was asking.

"If I thought someone had a reason to kill me, any kind of reason at all, I would have been more suspicious about that phone call this morning. I—" She shook her head. "There *was* something sort of familiar about his voice, but I've been spending so much time talking to police officers lately, I thought that was it. And I didn't recognize Pleasance's voice when she called, so I was a little off-kilter, anyway."

"You had another call this morning?"

"Just Pleasance Geary, calling to tell me her granddaughter's sick and won't make it to softball practice."

"Is there anything you've ever been involved in that might make you a target? Drugs, even back in high school?" She was already shaking her head, but he held up a hand. "Think carefully. This fellow is serious. If you've held anything back from me, you need to tell me now. How about the people in your life? Your family, your sister, an ex-boyfriend?"

"No, no, and no. My sister won't pollute her body with anything harder than white wine, and my love life is dead and buried—or at least moved to Arizona, which is close enough—and I don't—"

He saw the effort she made to draw herself in.

"I know you have to ask these questions, Daniel. But I've never even gotten a parking ticket. Well, I did once, but that was because Rachel, my college roommate, had borrowed my car, and—" She caught herself again.

"Nothing like this has ever happened to me. Not before last Friday night, anyway," she finished, her composure cracking.

His own over-involvement be damned; he'd met enough accomplished liars to know Destiny Millbrook didn't qualify. She was clean. And if someone close to her was involved in any criminal activity, she didn't know about it.

If he could no longer trust his instincts, it was time to find another line of work.

"Friday night, then," he said. He pulled out his notebook, flipping to his notes on the case. "In the past week you've been mugged in the park, had a possible break-in at your house, and been shot at with a high-powered rifle. Coincidences do happen, but that's pushing it."

"Do you think—" Her voice failed, and she began again. "Do you think it could be the same guy? The one who tried to choke me in the park?"

"It's possible the incidents are related. Are you sure your caller this morning mentioned a hooded sweatshirt?"

She nodded.

"That information wasn't in the police blotter in the paper."

He pushed back from the desk, his instincts drawing him on. "In fact, that attack Friday night and the sniper this morning may both be related to the break-in at your house."

Lars Holmgren had said it seemed as though the intruder knew where he was going. Which could mean nothing. But it could mean the man had targeted Destiny, knew she'd gone out walking the dog, and had planned to wait in hiding for her to return—until Holmgren prevented her from entering the house and called the police.

"Stalkers often make that kind of effort. . . ." Daniel shook his head. "But the rifle attack isn't consistent with a stalker. They like to confront their victims face-to-face."

Destiny's skin had paled to near transparency. "It's more like a contract killing."

"Which makes no sense—"

"Unless I'm somehow involved in drugs or something," she finished for him. "But I'm not. Unless Mr. Holmgren's running a meth lab in his basement. Our neighborhood is quiet. We get some transients at the library, but they're mostly older people who just want a place to sit awhile. I've never even witnessed a dope deal. . . ." She stopped, her eyes widening.

Daniel had arrived at the same thought. "The men you heard arguing in the park. If they thought you'd overheard a drug deal, one of them might have followed you to make sure

111

you didn't call the police."

"That's it!" Destiny agreed, half out of her seat. "That must be it. We've . . ." Her excitement faded. "But I *didn't* hear anything. At least nothing that would help us find them."

"You said they were arguing about money."

She bit her lip, her face twisted in frustration. "I got that impression. I just . . . It didn't really make any sense, but there was something about payment, I think. One of them, the louder one—he was the one who really sounded angry—said something like, 'That's not what I paid you for.' I couldn't hear the other guy very well, and I was trying not to eavesdrop, but he said something like, 'It worked, didn't it?' "

Her eyes met Daniel's, fierce. "If I'd known they were going to shoot at me later, I would have paid more attention."

"Would you recognize the voices if you heard them again?"

"Probably not. I wasn't paying attention. They were well educated, I'd guess. Like I said before, they didn't *sound* like drug dealers."

"You'd be surprised." Daniel took another look at his notes. "You said something odd on our walk through the park Saturday. That maybe they were talking about the railroad?"

Destiny's gaze focused inward as she strained for the memory. "That's right. They didn't *say* railroad, I'm pretty sure. But they were talking about an engine. And some kind of gauge. Don't railroads come in different gauges? Or is that just model trains?"

Daniel's scalp prickled, excitement and dread crawling up his spine. "I don't think they were talking about railroads." It was just a hunch, but it made a terrible sort of sense. "I don't think they were talking about a gauge at all. I think it was a name. Gage Barclay."

It fit. Heaven help them all, it fit.

Destiny's hands shook a little as she leaned forward. "The county supervisor who was killed in the plane crash?"

"Gage Barclay's plane crashed the same day you were attacked. As I said, coincidences do happen. But . . ."

"A plane has an engine. And if someone tampered with Gage Barclay's plane . . ." Destiny swallowed. "It wasn't a drug deal at all."

"The FAA inspector said pilot error caused the crash," Daniel said. "But there were plenty of people who weren't happy with his position on the ShopSmart development project." It might be time to get a voiceprint made of Fiona's tape.

He might have no suspects for a sniper attack on a law-abiding librarian, but he had a truckload of people who wanted to see Gage Barclay out of commission.

In just five minutes he'd gone from too few suspects to too many. As long as the perpetrators remained at large, Destiny remained in danger. The bullet to her tire might have been intended to make her death look like an accident, but the sniper had gone to another level when he'd fired directly at the two of them. Her assailant wouldn't waste time setting up "accidents" in the future.

"Daniel?"

He realized he'd been staring at the wall. Destiny had put down her coffee cup and huddled in her chair, the gray tinge to her skin more exhaustion than fear. She looked painfully vulnerable.

"Yes?"

"May I go home now?" She smiled weakly. "All my adrenaline's gone. I think I need a hot bath and a cup of tea. Or maybe a shot of bourbon."

"Destiny, you can't go home." At the expression on her face, he crossed to the other side of the desk to crouch beside her chair. "They know your name. They know your phone number. They know where you live."

As he watched the words reawaken her terror, he took her hand, her slender fingers cold in his.

"I feel like I'm in a Robert Ludlum thriller." Her voice shook only a little. "Are you going to stash me in a safe house?"

"Hope Point doesn't have the budget for a safe house." He was glad to hear her attempt at humor. "But I think it would be best for you to move in with your sister for a few days."

"And put her in danger, too? No way."

He shook his head, his voice calm. "She kept her married name, didn't she? They won't make the connection to you."

"How do you know?" she demanded. "That guy couldn't have gotten a much better look at me than I did at him last Friday night, but he managed to track me down."

Her hands trembled, and he wished he could restore her sense of safety.

"He must know I work at the library. On Monday, Maddy said that someone was calling, trying to get my name. . . ." She gulped air, struggling for calm.

"Listen to me," Daniel said, rubbing her fingers between his. "This is not a Ludlum novel. You'll be safe; I'll make sure of it. We'll have a security detail watching your sister's house—"

"I have a twelve-year-old niece. I am *not* going to put Sarah in danger. I'll stay in a hotel room or something."

"Once they figure out you're not at home, the area hotels will be the first place they'll look. It comes down to this: Unless you want to live in my office until we catch these men, you'll have to trust us to protect you at your sister's. The only other 'safe house' I can think of would be a police officer's home."

She snatched her hand from his and stood, her lips tight. He rose with her. He didn't like pressuring her, but he was telling her the truth. Besides, he would personally insure the safety of her sister and niece when she moved in with them.

"All right."

Daniel's chest relaxed. He'd feared she wouldn't recognize the inevitable. He appreciated her strength, admired it, but . . .

"Do you have a fenced yard?"

"What?"

She frowned impatiently. "A fenced yard. Do you have one? For Fleur."

"Fleur?" She'd lost him. "I can't take Fleur. I have a cat."

He thought he heard her mutter, "I knew it."

She smiled at him, the way his mother had smiled when she'd insisted he eat his green beans. "A cat's okay. Fleur loves cats."

Daniel pictured the big, eager Lab chasing Edgar around his house and felt the first stirrings of panic. "Why can't you take Fleur to Serena's with you?"

Her smile, if possible, became even more formidable. "I'm not moving in with Serena. I'm moving in with you."

Destiny sat silently in the passenger seat of the replacement vehicle the department had assigned Daniel, watching wisps of mist blow up into the saplings alongside the road. A breeze had begun as they left the Hope Point Police Station and was clearing patches of blue over the slate-colored sea.

But she couldn't bring herself to gaze at the ocean. The memory of her car skidding toward the cliff edge remained too vivid. Even the thought of it shot a jolt of adrenaline into her throat and quickened her breathing.

She couldn't reach for Daniel's strength to steady her this time, either. She would be fine all by herself, thank you very much. Still, it would be nice to know that he wasn't privately wishing her car had flipped over the cliff after all.

The situation wasn't her fault. She'd made the only possible decision, under the circumstances. If some idiot wanted her dead, she had to stay as far away from Serena and Sarah as possible.

But with Daniel stiff and frowning beside her and with Fleur in the back seat already fragrancing the little Ford with the musty smell of dog, returning to her own home almost seemed worth the risk. At least Fleur wasn't leaving yellow hairs all over Daniel's regular unmarked car—the Chevy was at the station being searched for rifle slugs.

Daniel slowed, taking the turnoff for Shell Creek. Tourism and wealthy retirees had brought an influx of money to the small harbor town, but its clapboard houses, faded and softened by wind and salt spray, retained the flavor of its halcyon days as a fishing village. Daniel turned down a narrow lane that ran south of town, through spruce and pine toward the sea.

The last house on the lane was more of a cottage; a low-slung building of weatherworn cedar that blended with the bluff grass and had a view of Cypress Head across the tiny bay. A high redwood fence stretched behind the house to the cliff's edge. Destiny was almost sure that Fleur had enough sense not to leap off a thirty-foot cliff.

Daniel pulled the department car into the driveway beside an old, battered Toyota truck. His own vehicle did not appear to be a huge improvement over his work car.

Destiny climbed out of the Ford and breathed the ocean smell of salt and fish. "This is a beautiful spot."

"It's all right." Daniel's wry smile eased her nerves a little.

He opened the car's rear door, and Fleur hopped out, her body taut with excitement at the smell of the sea.

"I'll put her in the backyard," Destiny said, moving toward the gate. "Let her settle down a bit before we inflict her on your kitty."

"Cat. Edgar is a cat." He grabbed her bags from the trunk and strode toward the front stoop. Destiny left Fleur exploring the yard and followed him.

The inside of the cottage matched the outside for functional simplicity yet welcomed her with an impression of quiet comfort. A stone fireplace dominated the sunken living room, which looked out through floor-to-ceiling windows toward the ocean. To the left, the kitchen-dining room area was separated from the living room by a partial wall that dropped into a counter as it stretched toward the back door. To the right, a hallway ran down to the other rooms. Thick beige carpeting muffled their footsteps, and striking Navajo rugs decorated the walls.

"Did you buy these?" Destiny asked, lifting her fingers to a huge rug in a Two Grey Hills pattern.

"My parents retired to New Mexico. I save my money for visits at Christmas."

"I'll say." He certainly didn't spend money on his truck.

"Let's put your stuff in my room and—"

"No, please. I won't take your room." She already felt guilty about intruding on his life.

"There's a futon in my study," he continued. "And you can't have my study."

He met her gaze with that bland look that didn't hide the challenge and humor in his eyes. She shook her head, conceding victory.

As she followed him down the hall, she wondered if she

should have hung back a moment, giving him time to tidy up, remove stray underwear lying on the floor. But, stepping through the bedroom door, she realized she needn't have worried. He'd even made his bed that morning.

"I bet I could run a finger across your windowsill and not come up with dust," she accused, forcing her attention away from the large four-poster with its masculine black and brown woven blanket.

"I have to be careful. I never know when a beautiful woman is going to insist on moving in with me."

He set down her suitcase and overnight bag and tugged the curtains closed. She knew he did it to keep out prying eyes, knew it should send a shiver of fear up her spine. But in the sudden gloom, the shiver she experienced didn't feel much like fear.

"I'll leave you to settle in," he said, and she nodded without looking at him, because the sound of his voice felt like velvet on her ears. "You can have the top couple of drawers in the dresser there; just shove my stuff down below. There should be room. Do you think you could eat anything?"

The constant, niggling guilt erupted again. "You don't have to feed me, too."

"That's right. I've sold out to the bad guys. I was supposed to lure you out to my house and then starve you to death. The perfect plan."

She frowned at him, hand on her hip. "All right, Parks, I'll eat. But no ketchup, or I'm charging you with police brutality."

"Duly noted."

He left her alone in his bedroom. She opened her overnight bag. She kept it ready for spur of the moment weekend camping trips with Fleur, and it was well stocked. Usually she'd forgotten she needed a new stick of deodorant, but she seemed to have enough to last a pro basketball team a couple of months.

She approached the suitcase with more trepidation. Daniel had sent Kermit Riggs to pick up additional clothing from her house, and she expected to find he'd forgotten to pack socks or had filled the bag with winter blazers. But to her surprise, the assortment of clothes looked well balanced. He'd even packed her comfy old sweats with the paint drips and bleach stains. And that horrible fuchsia-colored sweat-shirt her mom had sent her last Christmas.

She intended to unpack and settle in as Daniel had suggested. But as she sat down on the edge of the bed to open the first drawer, she suddenly felt as though she'd been run over by an eighteen-wheeler.

The room danced a little before her eyes, and when she put a hand on the bed to steady herself, she could feel the mattress calling her. She put another hand down to push herself up, but the bed was like the tarbaby in the Br'er Rabbit story; the more she struggled, the more it pulled her in.

She heard Daniel's voice from the kitchen, talking to his cat. Maybe she could lie down for a few minutes before helping him with lunch. She'd just take off her running shoes and lie back . . . but the room was a little cool after the morning fog.

Feeling like a bear kept from hibernation too long, she slipped out of her jeans and burrowed under the covers. The bed didn't have the familiar lumps and valleys of her mattress at home, but she decided she could live with that as it enveloped her in somnolent warmth.

She buried her face in the pillow, and as her breathing slowed, she realized the pillowcase held the faint scent of Daniel's aftershave. The thought burned her skin, and it briefly occurred to her that staying with Daniel could be more dangerous to her peace of mind than the bad guys taking pot-shots at her.

Still, she couldn't escape the sense of security she felt in his home, in his bed, as exhaustion pulled her down into sleep.

Edgar sat in the kitchen window staring at Daniel, determinedly keeping his back to the big yellow beast he did *not* see snuffling about in the yard.

"Don't start, Edgar," Daniel warned, dialing the station phone number. "At least she's not going to be sleeping in your bed."

Amber eyes met his accusingly.

"That's *my* bed, Edgar. I'll move your blanket into the study with me."

The cat landed on the tile floor with a thud and trotted stiff-legged down the hall to confront the human intruder in *his* room.

Daniel returned his attention to the phone. He wouldn't think of Destiny being in his bedroom. Putting her clothes in his closet. Sleeping in his bed.

Nancy Dennis's voice at the other end of the line distracted him.

"Hi, Nance, Daniel here. Any news?"

"Lieutenant Marcy complained to the chief about your stealing Kermit from Patrol Division to go on protection duty for the next few days. Lieutenant Tiebold promised you'd make it up to him."

Daniel groaned. "I'm sure I will. How about my sniper?"

"Not good. Your perp evaded the CHP's roadblock."

"About what I expected. Thanks, Nancy. You know where to reach me." He hung up. Exactly what he'd expected. But it would have been nice if they'd caught the guy. Nice to see the relief on Destiny's face when he told her. Nice to get rid of the fear that had lodged under his ribs when he realized someone wanted to kill her.

This is a case, Parks. A touchy one. Focus on the danger at all times.

Which would be much easier if Destiny were ensconced at her sister's and he was trading shifts in a cold, uncomfortable surveillance car out front. He should have insisted. Shouldn't have agreed to her coming here, where the image of her arose in his mind too easily. Her skeptical eyes glinting. Her skin glowing with warmth, her lip caught between her teeth . . .

He breathed deeply. This was going to be hell. Pure hell. To have her here, wanting to touch her. Wanting her.

No denying it. He did want her. He'd known it when she'd cried in his arms this morning at the side of the highway while some nut pinned them in his rifle sights. Knew it now, with her just down the hall.

And he'd learn to live with it. Because he couldn't send her to her sister's. She was safer here. Here there would be no security detail for a killer to follow to the house. Even if the killer connected her to her sister or niece, it wouldn't help him find her here. No other part of her life connected her to Daniel.

Just as it should be. And he wouldn't have to be home all the time. When he was out, Kermit would be here. And Kermit would be driving from home, not the police station. One fewer connection for a killer to follow.

Meanwhile, if someone did try to find Destiny at any of the local inns, he'd made a few phone calls that ought to direct the gunman astray and might even result in a lead or two for Daniel.

No, she hadn't forced him to let her stay here. It was the

best solution. She'd be safe here. Now if he could just protect himself from the danger to his equilibrium . . .

A scream ripped through the afternoon peace, piercing his heart with dread. There was no mistaking its source. It had come from his bedroom.

Chapter 8

Daniel's hand fumbled from unfamiliar fear as he pulled his gun from the shoulder holster he'd slung over the back of a chair. He heard another cry, muffled this time, and bit back a shout of his own as he sprinted down the hall.

He'd been congratulating himself on how safe Destiny was, and someone had reached her here, in his own home. If anything happened to her . . .

He slammed the bedroom door open with his shoulder. Crouched low, he held his gun up and ready as his gaze swept the room. In the gloom, movement caught his eye. Something on the bed.

Another screech tore the air, this one inhuman, loud and furious. A mass of fur, solid as a bowling ball, burst past him into the hallway, eyes wild.

Daniel's gaze returned to Destiny sitting upright in the bed, her eyes as wide as the cat's, her hair standing up around her head in a comic parody of terror.

"Oh!" she gasped. Slowly she focused on Daniel. "I think . . . I think I had a bad dream."

Daniel moved forward to sit on the edge of the bed, setting his gun on the night table. The weapon clattered as his hand shook. "I'm afraid that was Edgar."

He could see her tremble, but a faint smile turned her lips. "Poor thing. I don't think he liked it when I screamed."

Unthinking, Daniel reached out to brush the hair away from her cheek. Despite its wild curl, the stray lock was soft to the touch.

"I don't think you'll have to worry about his trying to share the bed again," he said.

"I'm sorry I fell asleep. I was just so tired after this morning, I thought—"

"You needed the rest." He could tell she hadn't completely shaken off the nightmare. Her eyes remained dilated and dark. "You should have said something. I'd have changed the sheets."

A spark of mischief returned to her expression. "You probably iron your sheets. I don't know if I could sleep in a bed with ironed sheets."

"As a matter of fact, I don't. So there." He smiled at her, but his mouth felt dry. Her words had brought home to him the fact that she was lying between his sheets. That she was the one who had rumpled the bedspread, that her scent mingled with his on his pillow. It was time to return to the kitchen, make some more phone calls. "So, you're all right?"

She smiled and nodded. But then her face crumpled, and she trembled again, and he could do nothing but reach for her, pull her close against his chest as she shook. Despite her distress, she was warm and soft with sleep, and her body molded against his.

He knew he should get up and walk away. But now that he had her in his arms, he couldn't let her go. He stroked her back, to comfort her, to reassure himself as much as her. He bent his head closer to her, the light scent of her hair filling his lungs.

Slowly, she tilted her head back to face him, to search his eyes for the answer to the question he saw in hers. Hesitantly, he lowered his mouth to hers.

Her lips tasted warm, soft, sweet and salty as a summer ocean breeze. The whisper of her throaty moan brushed against his mouth, and Daniel found himself drowning in the need to pull her closer. He tasted her with his tongue, and she met it with hers, the warm, gentle kiss a sudden heat flaring out of control.

His groan mingled with hers in the need between them. He couldn't remember the last time he had felt this way about anyone, the last time he had needed a woman's kiss as much as he needed air to breathe. There was only this moment, this woman, this kiss.

He stroked her face, drinking in the softness of her skin through his fingertips. Her hands found his hair, tugging as though he could kiss her more deeply than he already was. He could taste her need, and it fed his own until there was no difference between the kiss and desire.

Alarms rang in Destiny's head. Her attraction to Daniel was too fast, too strong. It fogged her logic. He wasn't her type. Too steady, too sensible. *Remember what happened the last time you ignored your good sense. What if he doesn't care for you the way you might be able to care about him?* But the blood pounding in her ears muffled the alarms.

Destiny knew she should stop now, before it went any further, before she no longer cared if they stopped. But she'd passed that moment, sometime before he'd ever kissed her.

Daniel slid his hands down her rib cage, and Destiny gasped, overwhelmed by her own response to his touch, the need to have him touch her.

She pressed herself to him, her breasts crushed to his chest, her breath panting into his mouth, and a kiss was nowhere near enough. His palm found her panties beneath the covers, the warm length of one bare leg. He brushed his thumb along the inside of her thigh, and she trembled.

Destiny dropped her head to his shoulder, struggling for control, struggling to breathe. Even as his hand stroked fire along her thigh, she brushed her lips up his neck, ran her tongue along the line of his jaw. Breath shuddered from him. "Destiny . . ."

Edgar's shrill, inhuman screech split the cocoon of desire that surrounded them. Something hit the back of the house with a force that made the walls shake.

Destiny swallowed a cry of her own. "What was that?"

She had felt Daniel's body tense, prepared for danger, but then he relaxed, a shadow of a smile shading his mouth. "I think Fleur just discovered that Edgar's cat door isn't big enough for a Labrador retriever."

"Clumsy dog," Destiny said, not knowing whether to laugh or sob. For in that reminder of peril, Daniel, though he still had a protective hand on her shoulder, had pulled away. The physical distance was almost imperceptible, but she knew that the distance in his eyes could not be bridged.

"Destiny, I . . ." His hand stopped before it touched her cheek. "I'm sorry."

"I know." She tugged the covers up and averted her eyes. "This isn't a good idea."

"No, it's not. When you screamed, I thought—" He took a heavy breath. "We've both been under a lot of stress lately. And with the danger we faced this morning . . ."

"You're saying this was just a reaction to stress." Her voice sounded strange in her own ears.

"Yes. Stress and . . ." His voice trailed off as he stood. "I'm supposed to be protecting you. I shouldn't have taken advantage. It won't happen again."

"I didn't feel taken advantage of." It required all her courage to say it with a smile, but he didn't smile back.

"I can't protect you if I let personal considerations interfere." He picked his gun up off the table. His eyes met hers. "And protecting you has to be my only priority."

She thought he might say something else, but a knock at

the front door had him turning away. He tucked his gun into his belt. "Destiny? I don't want you to get killed."

And he was gone, closing the door behind him. So she could get dressed. Her legs shook as she slid off the bed and reached for her jeans. No, not her tight jeans. She fumbled through the suitcase Kermit had packed and dragged out her old sweats.

She should have known better. Should have known to hide her feelings until she was certain of his. But she'd been swept away by his desire, mistaking it for something else. She couldn't blame him for it. He did care about her; he wasn't the kind of guy to kiss someone for kicks. He simply didn't care enough.

"The story of my life."

Why did she keep falling for men who didn't want her?

Embarrassed and angry, she pushed the thought aside. Which left her trying not to cry.

She heard footsteps in the hall and knew she had to face Daniel sometime. Soon. Had to pretend his rejection didn't hurt, pretend she believed it was for her own good. But couldn't he have given her a few minutes to get over her desire to disembowel him? To get over her desire . . .

"Dess?" Serena opened the door and slipped through without knocking, her model-smooth skin wrinkled with worry. "Oh, honey, are you okay?"

Serena hugged her, and it felt good to be a little sister again for just a minute.

"I've been frantic since you called from the police station. You're not hurt? You're sure?"

Destiny managed a smile. "Of course I'm sure. I'm fine."

Her sister held her at arm's length. "Baby, you're not fine. You look awful."

"Thanks a lot!"

"If your sister can't tell you the truth, who can?" Serena looked her up and down again. "Daniel read me the riot act for coming up here, but I had to see you for myself. You sounded wiped out when you called me. You're sure you're okay? You look like you've been crying."

"I just woke up. I had a bad dream."

"Why don't you splash some water on your face. You'll feel better," Serena suggested.

She followed Destiny into the hall, leaning in the doorway to the bathroom. "I stopped by the library and brought you some books. Maddy said to tell you to buck up. She said four or five patrons have already asked why you're not at work today."

"What did she tell them?" Destiny asked, panicking.

"That a gorgeous, wealthy, very distant cousin whisked you away to Monaco for the rest of the week."

"That sounds like Maddy, all right." She should have known Maddy would find an improbably romantic cover story for her absence.

"She said a couple of the curious patrons were very cute guys. Maybe I should mention that to Daniel."

"Reenie, don't. Just don't."

Serena sobered again. "Are you going to be all right out here? Do you want me to stay with you? I could take Sarah down to Santa Rosa to her father's for a few days."

"Thanks, Reenie, but I'll be fine. I'm hoping it won't take long for the police to catch the bad guys." The cold water felt good on her skin, washing away the burn of embarrassment.

"I'd like to get a shot at the dirty—" Serena stopped herself. "Sorry. I'm trying to keep calm about this, especially in front of Sarah. I couldn't tell her you'd been shot at. The sooner they catch this creep, the better."

Her deep concern gave way to a sly smile that was pure

Serena. "Of course, I can think of worse things than being holed up with a gorgeous cop whose only desire is to keep you safe."

"It might be okay if that weren't his *only* desire," Destiny muttered, examining her reflection in the bathroom mirror. She *did* look awful.

"Hah! I knew it!"

"Knew what? Do you have a comb?"

Serena pulled a comb from her purse. "Knew you'd fall for Detective Daniel Parks, given half a chance. 'He's not my type.' Baloney."

"I have *not* fallen for Daniel Parks," Destiny said, realizing in the vehemence of the statement that it was a lie. "And, anyway, he certainly hasn't fallen for me. So you can put away your matchmaking plans."

"You should have seen the look on his face when he saw me on the stoop, 'endangering your life.' "

"He's the one who said I should be staying at your house!"

"Apparently he's changed his mind." Serena dug around in her purse. "Here. A little powder on your nose won't hurt. Anyway, I left my car at Jesse's house and drove his truck. Nothing to connect me to you. And even if the bad guys find out you're staying with Daniel, they'll probably never find this place. I almost didn't. I should have asked directions when you gave me the address. Anyway, your detective was ready to string me up before I had a chance to explain."

"He was doing his duty." The words felt dry in her throat.

Serena snorted. "Try some lip gloss. And where did you get that idea?"

"He told me so himself." There. She'd said it. "So maybe I did take a chance, Reenie. And he told me he wants to keep this as just a case."

"Uh-huh." Serena took back her lip gloss. "You know that

man takes his job too seriously."

"Serena, I'm not going through that again. I deserve better than being in a relationship with someone who's not in a relationship with me."

"Of course you do," her sister said. "It's time you believed that, Desty. Don't let that SOB what's-his-name determine what you think about yourself. He was an idiot. Daniel's not."

"You hardly even know Daniel."

"The tarot—"

"Serena."

Her sister shrugged. "I'm very perceptive about people, all right? You look much better. Though I'd suggest you change out of those awful sweats."

"It's not going to make a bit of difference."

"Of course not." Serena smiled. "You could probably drag yourself out of a mud flat and Daniel would still drool. Come to think of it, he and Fleur would make a good pair."

Destiny laughed. Serena was irrepressible.

"That's better. You look even prettier when you laugh. Now let's go see how crazy we can drive that detective of yours while he tries to do his duty."

It was Friday before Daniel admitted to himself that Destiny and her sister might well drive him right out of his mind.

Over the past two days Destiny had acted with a polite formality he didn't know how to respond to. Of course, his reaction to her warmth and openness had been a disaster, so he couldn't exactly fault her.

He had acted like an idiot, coming on to her like some movie cop or a rookie who didn't know any better. The feelings she brought out in him rose like floodwater in spring, uncontrollable, dangerous. Maybe he was afraid of them. He should be. They could get her killed.

Or break his heart.

They'd already hurt his growing friendship with her, maybe damaged it beyond repair.

As for her sister, Serena had not returned to his house after lunch on Wednesday, respecting his request to keep Destiny isolated from any connection to her regular life that the perps might follow. Instead, Serena called five or six times a day, spending as much time interrogating him as she did talking to Destiny. She'd spent twenty minutes that morning alternating between grilling him about the case and making "innocent" inquiries about how he and Destiny had spent the evening before.

He hoped he'd managed to hide his relief when Kermit showed up to replace him as bodyguard and he could escape to his office. He'd thrown himself into the routine. The sooner he found out who was behind the attempt on Destiny Millbrook's life, the sooner she could move back to her own home and the sooner he could return to his quiet, solitary life.

If he got her out of his house soon enough, he might not even notice how lonely it would be without her.

He'd told Kermit he'd be back by five-thirty, and it was nearly six now, but he still had one more stop to make. He hadn't made much positive progress over the past forty-eight hours, but he had eliminated several potential suspects by confirming their alibis for the time Destiny's car had been fired on.

That left only about ten or fifteen other Salton Enterprises lawyers, contractors, company reps—or their accomplices— as serious contenders. He hadn't mentioned to anyone the reason for his new round of questioning, but he had the gut feeling that he'd made at least one or two people very nervous during the course of the afternoon. Criminals tripped themselves up when they got nervous.

He pulled into Fiona Barclay's driveway. She met him at the door herself, her spun-silk hair tied in a ponytail with a black bow. She looked more like the high school girl he remembered than a wealthy widow in mourning. Dark smudges still haunted her eyes, but her step was strong as she led him to the living room.

As her brother, Philip, rose to greet him, Daniel's gaze moved to the third person in the room, a slender brunette with feminine curls and a soft, rounded face that hid a will of steel.

"Hello, Daniel."

"Hello, Tessa." He waited for the wave of sorrow that usually hit him when he ran into his ex-wife. It didn't come.

"Tessa thought a civil suit might be my best option, depending on what you'd found," Fiona explained. "So I invited her to hear what you have to say."

Tessa and Fiona were close friends; he could hardly ask Tessa to leave.

"I don't know who made those threatening telephone calls to Gage," he began, taking a seat. "But another incident has occurred which suggests there may be more to those calls than mere harassment."

"Gage's death?" Fiona asked.

"I've spoken at length with the FAA inspector. He says it's nearly impossible to sabotage a plane so that it takes off without incident and then crashes later without leaving telltale evidence behind. But this new incident is compelling enough that I'd like to have your permission to ask the coroner to perform some additional tests on your husband."

He admired Fiona's calm. She paled, but her voice remained steady. "You want to exhume the body."

"For God's sake, Daniel. How could you?" Philip stood, his eyes dark.

Fiona took Tessa's hand. "Philip, let him explain."

"The coroner ran the routine tests for drugs in Gage's system," Daniel said, his own voice even. "He didn't find anything suspicious. But I'd like to rule out other toxins not normally tested for."

Fiona's eyes closed. "Poison."

"Look, Daniel, I'm sorry," Philip said. "I know you wouldn't ask Fee to endure this without a good reason. But you said yourself that Gage's death was an accident. I want her to put all this behind her."

"I won't, Philip," Fiona said. "Not until I know for sure what happened to Gage. Not until the people who murdered him pay for what they did."

Her green eyes shone as she looked at her brother. "Even if it means you lose money when the ShopSmart project is shut down."

"Blast it, Fee! You know I don't care about that. I just don't want you to keep hurting. And it's not just you. I got a call from Pleasance Geary today. I've never heard her voice shake like that, she was so upset about being questioned by the police. How many more people's lives have to be disrupted by this?" Philip stormed from the room. They heard him close the back door, too much a gentleman to slam it.

Fiona turned to Daniel. "You have my permission to do whatever needs to be done. I just . . . need to know. You'll call me?"

"Of course."

Her smile was small and tired. "I'd better find Philip. Gage's death hasn't been easy on him, either."

Fiona slipped out, and Daniel was left alone with Tessa. She smiled the soft little smile that caused the witnesses she cross-examined to blanch with fear.

"You handled that well," she said.

"Thank you."

"I should have known you'd know how to handle Fiona to get what you wanted."

"We've been divorced over a year and half, Tessa. Maybe it's time we stopped picking fights every time we meet." He stood, reaching for his car keys.

She rose, too. "I'm not picking a fight. I know how cops think—I lived with you for five years, remember? In a murder case, your first suspects are the grieving family members."

His keys weren't in his pants pocket.

"Most victims are killed by people close to them. You know that, Tessa." Not in either pocket, not lost in the chair he'd been sitting in.

"Well, you can jolly Fiona along with your good-hearted family friend routine, but I'm going to be here with her, and I'm not going to let you do anything to jeopardize her rights. She's a victim here, Daniel, not a suspect. What on earth are you doing?"

"Looking for my car keys. I don't consider Fiona Barclay a suspect. In anything. All right?"

"Cross your heart? Did you check your pants pockets?"

He looked at her. Her smile might even be genuine. "Cross my heart. Yes, I checked my pants pockets."

He stuck a hand into his jacket pocket. Pay dirt. He pulled out his key chain, and a thin bit of silver dropped to the plush white carpet.

"What's that?"

He picked it up. Diamonds glittered. "A money clip." He'd forgotten all about it. Destiny would never believe that he could be so absent-minded about anything—even if it was unrelated to his caseload. "I must have stuck it in my jacket pocket when I returned to the station the other day."

"Since when do you make enough money to afford a diamond-studded money clip?" She took the piece from his hand.

"I found it in the park. I've been meaning to put an ad in the paper to try to find the owner."

He reached for it, but Tessa pulled her hand away.

"Wait. I recognize this." She turned it in her palm. "Yes, it's the same. Do you remember Barris Williams? He's in the corporate division of my firm."

"I recognize the name. He's the local attorney for Salton Enterprises." Barris Williams had come up during his investigations that very morning. But even then, there had been something familiar about the name, almost a sense of déjà vu.

"You must have met him at some office function or other. I'm sure I introduced you at the mayor's Christmas party a couple of years ago."

"Probably." It would explain why he didn't remember the man. That miserable Christmas party had occured right before he and Tessa had finally admitted they no longer had enough of a marriage to salvage. He hadn't thought it possible to get drunk on eggnog. He'd been wrong. Even now, the scent of nutmeg turned his stomach.

"You wouldn't forget Barris," Tessa assured him. "He's quite a character when he's drinking. Wispy white hair, stocky. He's got a bit of an accent; he was born in Wales."

An image clicked in Daniel's memory. "He dressed like he'd just walked off the set of a PBS production of a Charles Dickens novel or something."

Tessa's exasperated sigh didn't hide the smile in her eyes. "Not everyone can pull off the suave sophistication of a plain-clothes cop. At least, not without accessories. This money clip belongs to Barris."

Chapter 9

Daniel stared at his ex-wife. "Are you sure?"

"It's a distinctive design. He let me take a close look when I admired the clip after lunch one day. It's either his, or one just like it."

Daniel's scalp prickled. Coincidences happened, but . . . Finding a money clip belonging to a Salton Enterprises lawyer in the park gazebo the morning after Destiny had been attacked could be a lot more than coincidence.

Another image nudged at him, a figure in a gray suit disappearing down a path as he and Destiny exited the gazebo. The figure had struck him as familiar then. Could it have been Barris Williams, back to hunt for his missing money clip?

The man with the flowers had warned someone against interrupting the cop in the gazebo. A man with something to hide might not want that cop to see him.

Tessa sighed. "It's the sort of thing that makes me almost wish I'd gone into corporate law. A new Lexus and a time-share in Tahiti would almost compensate for the boredom. Of course, not every corporate lawyer can go out and buy pretty gewgaws like this money clip. Philip practically drooled over it at that luncheon. Fiona and Gage were there, too. Fee promised Philip she'd buy him one just like it for his birthday."

The excitement in Daniel's stomach twisted into something darker. "Did she?"

"What?"

"Get Philip a clip like this."

Tessa's eyes narrowed at his sharp tone. "I don't know.

136

We can ask right now, if we can find him."

"No, leave him with Fiona." He would follow up on that possibility himself if the clip did not belong to Barris Williams.

Tessa bounced the money clip on her palm. "I can take this to Barris for you if you'd like. I'm going into the office tomorrow morning anyway, and I'm sure he'll be working weekends until this ShopSmart deal is wrapped up."

Daniel shook his head.

"Thanks, Tessa, but I wanted to stop by to see him myself. Part of this investigation for Fiona. As the local lawyer for Salton Enterprises, he probably knows more than anyone about the intricacies of the development project." If he remained casual, she'd forget all about the clip, and he could surprise Barris Williams with it in the morning.

Tessa raised an eyebrow at him. "And it won't hurt to have his undying gratitude for rescuing this bit of finery, either. All right, you found it; you deserve the credit."

She handed him the clip, and he tucked it back into his pocket.

"Thanks." He hefted his keys, then paused. "I'm glad you're here with Fiona. She's got Philip, but—"

"He can be a little overprotective."

"Exactly. It . . . It was good to see you, Tessa." He found the sentiment was genuine. "Take care of yourself."

"Daniel?" Her voice stopped him at the door. "Are you feeling all right? Is something bothering you? You seem, I don't know . . ."

"Distracted?" He'd thought he'd hidden it well.

"No." She tilted her head as she examined him. "More human. Less like Robocop."

The comment brought back arguments he didn't want to relive. "Great. See you, Tessa."

"No, Danny, really." She stopped him again. "I wasn't trying to start a fight. I . . . I ran into Kerry Riggs at the grocery store yesterday." She paused, hunting for words, something he wasn't used to seeing her do. "He said you'd met someone."

As soon as he got home, he would strangle Kermit. "It's none of his business."

"Or mine." She shrugged. "But I like the change I see in you, Daniel. Don't let your job drive her away."

The old anger was still around after all. "Quit the sanctimonious garbage, Tessa. Your career was the one that was more important than our marriage."

Her full lips hardened. "I plan to learn from my mistakes. How about you?"

Daniel watched her turn and stalk out. She'd always had to have the last word. Maybe he had learned something, because he no longer did.

"I should have known you wouldn't do things by the book."

The statement brought Destiny's mind back from the wilds of Alaska and the Dana Stabenow mystery she was reading. Edgar shot her a warning glare from one baleful eye.

"No, I'm not getting up," she assured the feline.

He blinked skeptically and settled back into her lap. The cat had reason to feel safe there. Fleur had taken up residence on Daniel's couch and refused to lift her head from Kermit's thigh.

Kermit pointed to the *Choose the Perfect Pooch!* book Destiny had lent him. "You said this book helped you pick out Fleur."

"It did. I used it to figure out what kind of dog would fit best into my life."

"This book says that if you buy a purebred puppy, you can meet the parents, and if you know the temperament of the breed, you'll have a good idea of the personality of your dog. But you got Fleur at the Humane Society."

"That's true."

"So, was Fleur a surprise?" At the sound of her name, Fleur's tail dragged back and forth across Daniel's black and tan couch cushions. She gazed up at Kermit in adoration.

"Absolutely." Destiny had gotten Fleur soon after Alain left, to combat her loneliness. She'd gotten much more than she bargained for. "I researched Labrador retrievers, and I asked the people at the Humane Society all about Fleur. I took her for a walk and tried some of the temperament tests I'd read about."

Destiny smiled at the memory. "But the reality was still a surprise. I could have gone to a breeder and bought a show-quality Lab with parents of impeccable temperament, and I still wouldn't have been prepared for the changes she's brought into my life."

Kermit looked down at the patently un-show quality Lab beside him and gently rubbed between her eyes. "But you would have access to her genetic history. You would know your puppy's parents didn't have hip dysplasia."

"Yep."

He looked at her, expecting more.

"You've got time to think about all that, Kermit. First you have to decide for yourself what you want, what sorts of activities you plan to do with your dog. I didn't really want a little puppy, and I didn't care about showing my dog. But I knew the traits I wanted, and I didn't take a dog home until I found Fleur. It's been a struggle occasionally, but I couldn't ask for a better companion."

"I suppose that means you wouldn't let me take her home

with me." He managed to look almost as mournful as Fleur did when Destiny refused to share dinner with her.

Destiny realized with surprise that not only was Kermit teasing her, but he hadn't so much as tripped over a doorsill all day.

"You don't have a home to take her to, Kermit," she said with a mock scowl, enjoying the camaraderie that had developed between them over the past two days. "She's not an apartment dog."

"You could have my place, and I could stay here with Daniel."

"If someone starts shooting at you, then we'll talk."

Kermit laughed and picked the book up off the coffee table. Destiny smiled, too, but the exchange left her unsettled. The thought of leaving Daniel's house brought a huge sense of relief. She could hardly sleep at night; she couldn't stop thinking about being in Daniel's bed and about Daniel sleeping down the hall. If she left, she might get a decent night's rest.

And yet . . .

Fleur heard the telltale rattle of Daniel's old department Chevy, but her only sign was a perking of her ears toward the front door. Anything else would have required her to lift her chin from Kermit's knee.

"Give her a push, quick," Destiny urged from her armchair. "I bet Daniel has some silly rule about no dogs on the couch."

"Hey, girl," Kermit murmured, bending his long torso over the dog. "Time to get up now."

Fleur sighed and settled more comfortably into the cushions.

"Fleur, off!" Destiny ordered.

The dog sent her a baleful look. Destiny set down her book

with a threatening glare, and Fleur sagged off the couch. With a huff, the Lab turned her back on her human tyrant, which was just as well. Destiny feared Edgar might do her thighs permanent damage if Fleur surprised him with a big wet dog nose in his face.

Kermit had moved to the side of the doorway, ready for danger despite the sound of the key in the lock. Oblivious to the etiquette of a safe house, Fleur followed him, happily licking Daniel's hand as he walked through the door.

"Hello, dog."

Destiny noted that he absentmindedly paused to scratch beneath the Lab's chin. Fleur's heavy tail thumped against the door approvingly.

Destiny picked up her book, trying to keep her eyes off Daniel as Kermit filled him in on their afternoon. It didn't take long. After a wave to Destiny and a good-bye tussle with Fleur, Kermit slipped out into the cool, starry twilight.

And Destiny was left alone with Daniel.

"Have you eaten?" Destiny asked, pleased to find herself capable of mundane conversation after dreading—anticipating?—his return all afternoon. "Kermit and I used all our collective cooking skills and managed to whip up some hamburgers."

Daniel's gaze was far away, his tired smile distracted. "That sounds fine."

She heard him clattering in the kitchen, and half expected him to eat in there, avoiding her. But he brought his plate into the living room, taking Kermit's place on the couch.

Fleur sat by his knee, saliva pooling on her tongue as she gazed at his hamburger.

"Down," Daniel ordered. Fleur edged herself onto the floor, taking care to keep her jaw pressed close to his leg where he couldn't forget her. Daniel tore off a bite of burger, which Fleur took gently from his fingers and then swallowed with great jaw-wrenching chomps.

Fleur glanced at Destiny to see if she'd noticed.

"You'll never get rid of her now," Destiny warned.

"Ignoring her didn't seem to be working, either." He took a bite of hamburger, shared another with Fleur.

"I'm sorry to force Fleur on you, too." Destiny shook her head, not liking the hint of self-pity in the statement. "I mean, she's so big. Not exactly easy to adjust to if you're not used to dogs."

"I used to have a dog. I didn't get custody."

Destiny closed her eyes. She'd like to do one thing right with this man. She'd forced her way into his house against his wishes, forced her dog on him when he'd lost his own dog to his ex-wife. She'd made a fool of herself kissing him. Now if Fleur would chew up his favorite pair of slippers, she'd have a perfect record.

"I have a lead," Daniel said, unaware of her discomfort, his gaze still far away.

She spent a futile minute waiting for him to elaborate. "A lead?" she prompted.

He slipped Fleur another bite of burger. "You remember that money clip we found at the park last Saturday?"

She saw the flash of silver in his hand. "Oh, right. I'd forgotten all about it."

"Apparently it belongs to Barris Williams."

"The ShopSmart lawyer?" White hair, impish smile. He'd struck her as the absentminded professor sort. "Pleasance Geary introduced him to me at the library just this week. He seemed rather charming. What was his money clip doing in the park?"

And then it hit her, hard enough to knock her breath away. "You think he lost it there the night before? You think he might have been one of the men I overheard." She didn't want it to be true. "He might have lost it at a wedding or something, maybe weeks ago."

"Coincidences do happen, . . ."

"But." Destiny wrapped an arm around Edgar, needing the comfort of his fluffy solidity.

"Destiny, I can't be sure, but I might have caught a glimpse of him in the park that next morning, when you and I found the clip."

"If he was one of the two men I heard . . . If he saw us together, he must have known why we were there."

The theory of a murder conspiracy against County Supervisor Gage Barclay, even of a concerted plan to harm her, had, up until now, felt almost abstract, unreal. But to be able to picture the face of a man who might want her dead . . .

"Williams has an alibi for Wednesday morning," Daniel continued, his voice preventing her mind from skittering into the darkness opening around her. "I hadn't called him about it; I didn't seriously consider him a suspect. Lawyers get paid, whatever the outcome of a particular negotiation. But I did speak with several other people who said they were in a meeting all morning Wednesday, and his name was among the attendees."

It didn't help to know that Barris Williams was not the man shooting at her car Wednesday morning. That simply meant there was another man out there whose face she didn't know. A man who might still be searching for her.

Destiny shuddered. "That day, in the library, he seemed so thoughtful. Pleasance was about to go off on a tear, and he rescued me."

"Pleasance Geary?"

"Yes. They were going to talk about Salton Enterprises purchasing her land."

Daniel's eyes sharpened. "Pleasance Geary's name has come up frequently in this case. I've been told that my phone call questioning her about Gage nearly sent her into hysterics."

Destiny snorted. "I find that hard to believe."

"Destiny, are you certain the two voices you heard were both men?"

Destiny opened her mouth, but it took a moment for sound to emerge. "You don't . . . You couldn't think . . . That's ridiculous! Pleasance is a good woman. She would never do anything like that, not even if it meant the ShopSmart deal falling through. Not even . . ." Not even if the deal falling through ruined Pleasance's plans for her granddaughter's future?

"She has a gravelly voice," Daniel said. "Low for a woman."

"She has a cold!"

"When did you talk with her last?"

A chill crept through Destiny's veins. "She called Wednesday morning, right before the man who wanted me to drive out to Union Cove." She had been anxious to catch Destiny at home.

Destiny shook her head. "I don't believe it. I can't believe it. But . . . I didn't recognize her voice that morning . . ." Destiny's voice failed her.

She heard a clatter as Daniel set down his plate. He moved to the end of the couch to sit closer to her. "I'm sorry. I shouldn't have brought it up. It's not likely Pleasance Geary had anything to do with this. We won't talk about it again until I've had a chance to make sure she's not involved."

"No." Destiny pulled herself out of her anguished dread. "Please, Daniel, don't leave me out. I want to know. I don't want to think that somebody I know, or anyone at all, is trying to kill me. But I'd rather talk about it than pretend it's not happening."

"I know." He smiled his tired smile again, and suddenly his blue eyes were too close, the lines around his lips too familiar. "You're strong, and you have a quick mind. That's why I wanted to bounce ideas off you."

No doubt he also wanted them to be good friends. Destiny changed the subject. "How did you figure out the clip belonged to Barris Williams? Don't tell me it's inscribed 'To Barris, Love always, Mom' or something and we missed it."

"Not exactly." He held out the clip to her. It seemed only natural for her fingers to brush his as she took it from him. "We caught a lucky break. Tessa, my—" He faltered almost imperceptibly. "My ex-wife recognized it. Williams is a colleague of hers."

Destiny could think of nothing to say to that. He still sought out his ex-wife for advice on cases.

"Tessa was—I went up to—"

"You don't have to explain." The words rushed out, and then she was sorry. They sounded hurt, and she wasn't hurt. His life was his own business, none of hers. She tilted her face away to hide the red in her cheeks.

"I went up to see Fiona Barclay, Gage Barclay's widow," he continued, as though she hadn't spoken. "I don't know if you remember Philip Brooks—we ran into him in the park the same day we met Barris Williams. Fiona is Philip's sister. Tessa is a close friend of hers."

He reached over and took the money clip from her hand, the warmth of his fingers lingering on hers until she looked back at him. She thought at first that he didn't feel the electricity that passed between them at each brief contact, but, seeing his eyes, she realized he was taking a risk to connect with her.

"It was good, I think, to see Tessa. There's been a lot of animosity between us since well before the divorce. Maybe we've both decided that it's not necessary anymore." He turned the money clip in his hand, but she didn't think he saw it.

"It's sad, though, that we may never be friends again. We let our work interfere with our personal lives. It ruined our marriage, and it could have hurt my career."

Destiny began to understand that he was explaining why he was determined to keep his relationship with her strictly professional. Which gave her a strange sort of hope. Because the reason had nothing to do with her, while his telling her something so painful and personal had everything to do with her.

"Tessa was involved in one of your cases?" she asked.

"Not exactly. I met her while she was working in the District Attorney's office. She knew I was a cop. I thought she knew what that meant."

"She couldn't handle being married to a police officer?"

Daniel laughed without humor. "No more than I could handle being married to a lawyer. After we were married, she decided she needed a change. She became a defense attorney. Suddenly we were on opposite sides of the battle, every battle.

"She wanted information I couldn't share. I wanted her to be one of the 'good guys' again. Suddenly I was the hard-nosed, fascist cop, and she was the smooth-talking lawyer putting scum back on the street."

He slipped the money clip into his pocket. "It happened so fast, we never had a chance. I guess we each expected the other to be more loyal to us than to our jobs, and we were both disappointed."

He looked at her, his blue eyes somber. "I believe in what

146

I'm doing. I believe in justice. When I'm doing my job, that has to come first. Or I won't be able to believe in myself."

"I understand." And she thought that maybe she did. Maybe she understood just how much he'd already risked for her, believing in her innocence. "But I'd also never question your loyalty to those you care about."

He raised an eyebrow at her.

"The way you talked about Tessa right now. You're still protecting her. And there's Kermit. It means a lot to him that you trust and believe in him. I doubt too many people see past his awkwardness."

"Kerry's a lot sharper than he seems at first," Daniel said. "He's smart enough to use that to his advantage."

"Sort of like Columbo."

Daniel laughed. "You could say that."

"But he's cuter than Columbo."

Daniel's eyebrows did their knitting trick. "You mean like a puppy dog?"

She smiled blandly at him.

"It's the uniform, isn't it? I never should have changed to plain clothes."

"Plain clothes suit you just fine, Detective."

She hadn't meant to flirt with him. She couldn't seem to help herself. She wrenched the conversation back to her original subject.

"But you see, you just made my point for me. You stand behind the people you care about. I don't think you could be loyal to your beliefs if you weren't loyal to people, too. Maybe the conflict between the two isn't what you think it is."

She stopped, catching her lip with her teeth. "I'm sorry. I don't mean to intrude. It's just something I really . . . that I really respect about you. Loyalty is rare."

"Your love life? The one that moved to Arizona? Not that

147

it's any of my business." His eyes smiled at her. She hadn't convinced him, she could tell. But the strain had eased from his face.

"Alain?" She shrugged. "I thought maybe we'd get married and have a family. He thought maybe Sedona would nurture his creativity."

"You wouldn't go with him?"

"He never asked me to." She knew the old hurt rang in her voice, but she didn't care. "He told me he was going and that he'd call when he got there. He never called."

"Are you sure he ever arrived?"

"I got a card that Christmas advertising a pottery show he was part of. He'd scribbled, 'Love to see you there!' on it. In pencil."

Whatever she had expected, it wasn't for Daniel to laugh. Yet the gargling escaping his throat sounded suspiciously like suppressed laughter.

"I'm glad you find it humorous."

"I'm sorry. I was just picturing you showing up at the pottery show with your baseball bat. What an idiot that guy must have been."

"His mother said I scared him away with my self-reliance. This was back before my bride-of-Frankenstein hair, so maybe she was right."

"What's wrong with your hair?"

"Don't humor me, Parks."

"What?"

She stared at him. "You thought I did this on purpose?" She ran a hand through her tightly corkscrewing hair, leaving it sticking out at even wilder angles.

"The cashier at Harbor Books has blue and green streaks in her hair. Yours didn't strike me as odd."

"Oh." She pulled a strand forward and examined it

glumly. "So much for the bad-hair-day theory of why I haven't met the man of my dreams."

"Your hair didn't stop me from seeing how attractive you were the first time you walked into the station. And your self-reliance is part of what makes you beautiful."

"Stop. I don't need a pep talk," she said, embarrassed that she'd forced him into one.

"It's not a pep talk." The laughter had disappeared. "You are beautiful. Especially your eyes. I thought so even when I was hoping you were an escaped mental patient so I wouldn't have to begin an assault investigation at nine o'clock on a Friday night. I've met a lot of beautiful people. I've never met anyone quite like you."

As the words faded, his eyes grew distant again. "Look, it's late. Why don't you go to bed? We can talk in the morning."

Unable to think of a better response, Destiny forced a smile. "I don't know if I dare get up. Every time I move, Edgar growls at me."

"Edgar, that's no way to treat a guest."

One great amber eye deigned to blink in Daniel's direction.

"Don't worry about him. He's all bark. So to speak." Daniel stood and scooped Edgar off her lap, his hand brushing Destiny's leg. She turned her head to hide what she suspected showed in her eyes.

"Thanks. I really appreciate both of you for putting up with me and Fleur." She tried giving him a quick, light smile, but it faded on her lips.

Her gaze had surprised Daniel's with the distance stripped away, his eyes wary and hungry as a winter wolf's. Whatever she had been trying to hide, she saw it reflected in his eyes. Wanted to see it there, but couldn't be sure. Only a thin thread of pride stopped her from reaching for him.

Pride and the intrusion of a suspicious slurping sound into the evening silence.

"Fleur! Bad dog!" Daniel's hamburger had disappeared off the coffee table, along with half his deli potato salad. "Bad dog! Leave it!"

Fleur cringed, but her tongue slipped out for one more run at Daniel's plate.

Destiny lunged forward. At the last second, Fleur jumped out of her way, sending the heavy coffee table over with a thud that turned Edgar into a howling fury leaping out of Daniel's arms. Fleur scrambled over the couch after the cat with Destiny grabbing desperately for her tail. As Destiny tumbled to the floor, she heard Daniel yelling at Fleur, Edgar's strangled yowling, and another crash as both animals streaked for the bedroom, Daniel close behind.

Destiny stared at the ceiling. *So much for romance.*

Daniel hung up the phone, trying to rein in his frustration. It felt as though the receiver had been attached to his ear all day, and it had brought nothing but bad news.

He had looked forward to confronting Barris Williams that morning. He had planned to begin easily, an old acquaintance performing a favor by returning the money clip. By the way, do you know where you left it? When? What were you doing there? Moving into Tessa's version of him as hard-nosed cop.

Frightened men did stupid things.

With the ShopSmart development so close to a vote by the County Supervisors, Daniel had assumed Tessa would be right about Barris Williams being in his office, even on a Saturday. But the lawyer had flown to Houston before six that morning to meet with executives at Salton Enterprises headquarters. He wasn't expected back until tomorrow afternoon.

And since Kermit deserved a Saturday off, Daniel had been left to make phone calls and guard Destiny.

He felt like a caged beast. He hadn't become a police detective for the thrills and danger. *Good thing.* But still . . .

He glanced toward his living room. Destiny sat in his easy chair, her laptop teetering on her knees. She'd hooked into the library's computer system so she could work on interlibrary loans over the internet. She was the one who'd been stuck inside since Wednesday. With Fleur and Edgar, no less. Yet she'd maintained her serenity—mostly—and her sense of humor.

In just a few short days, she'd become a part of his home. In the mornings he smiled when he walked into the bathroom and found dog hair in the shower. He looked forward to coming home in the evening. He collected interesting stories to share with her.

He liked having her there. Liked spending time with her. If only he could stop noticing the softness of her lips, stop her scent from filling his head with roses and honey. He had to stop remembering the sight of her lying in his bed, her hands on his shoulders, her moans mingling with his.

Stir crazy. That's what he was. He moved into the living room and dropped onto the couch. If he felt this way after one day, how must Destiny feel? Edgar pushed onto his lap.

"What are you reading now?" Daniel picked the top book off the pile she'd left sprawled on the coffee table. "Nevada Barr. With a name like that, she'd have to write mysteries. Is it any good?"

"Yeah, but I've already read that one." Destiny leaned forward to look at the pile of books Serena had given Kermit to bring to her. "And that one. And that one. Haven't read this one yet."

She pushed it toward Daniel.

151

"*Jump Start Your Love Life Through the Power of Crystals.*"
He raised an eyebrow.

She shook her head. "After what happened with the full
moon, I think I'll pass. Maybe I'm a New Age jinx. My life
was better in a rut."

"How can you say that?" he asked. "Look what the moonlight brought you—an all-expense paid vacation at Parks's
Bed and Breakfast by the Sea."

"Dry cereal that I pour myself is hardly the breakfast ser-
vice I'd expect at such a fine establishment," she said. "And
the entertainment is sadly lacking."

"Breakfast—" No, no, *not* breakfast in bed, Parks. "—
Breakfast tomorrow will be the works. Eggs, bacon, you name
it. Nothing's too good for such an honored guest. And you're
welcome to borrow any of my books you'd like. I've even got
some mysteries. Lots of Robert Parker."

"Robert Parker, as in Spenser? Like *Spenser For Hire?*"

"I don't exactly picture the character as Robert Urich
played him."

Her eyes narrowed skeptically. "I'm not really into those
hard-boiled, sexist types."

"Give us a chance; we're not that bad."

She snorted. "The love life of crystals is starting to sound
pretty good."

Better than his love life at the moment. Cradling Edgar's
bulk with one arm, he rose and went to the bookcase by the
fireplace. "Here. *The Godwulf Manuscript.* It's the first
Spenser book."

She accepted it from him with obvious reluctance. "I'm
not really into heroes who have to prove their manhood with a
new girl in each book."

"Spenser's not like that. Now who's being sexist? What
about V. I. Warshawski and Kinsey Millhone? They haven't

exactly found true love and commitment."

"At least they're still looking."

She sounded so wistful. She probably didn't even realize it. His heart wanted him to reach for her. Sense told him to back off. He couldn't move, caught between the two.

"The search is the pits," he said. He wasn't even searching, and it was still the pits. "I guess you have to trust that the finding will make it worthwhile."

"It would certainly be worthwhile to have Serena off my back," she said. "But I'm not looking. If love wants me, he'll have to fall into my lap."

Don't tempt me. But she did. Tempted him badly. He could reach out to touch her chin, tilt her face toward his. "I—"

"Woof!" The coffee table jumped, spilling library books onto the floor, nearly sending Destiny's laptop flying along with them. Edgar howled, claws digging into Daniel's arms for purchase as he leaped for safety. Fleur heaved herself to her feet, undaunted by the table, her ears pricked, her tail whipping with delighted anticipation of a barking match with D'Artagnan next door.

"Down!" Daniel and Destiny ordered in unison. Fleur dropped with an anxious puff of air. In the relative silence, they heard the frantic yapping from the next yard.

"Doesn't that little fluffball ever stop barking?" Destiny asked, her first cross words about the poodle. "I'm about ready to muzzle it. Permanently."

Daniel felt similarly about Fleur at the moment. That dog had the worst timing. *No, best.* Best timing, Parks. She just saved your bacon. Be grateful.

"D'Artagnan's been excitable lately." Daniel moved toward the floor-to-ceiling windows that looked across his backyard to the sea. "A stray dog got into his yard and tried to eat him not long ago."

"There's an idea for breakfast," Destiny muttered, piling the books back onto the table. "Do you mind if I desert you and the rabid beasts to take a hot shower?"

She looked flustered, her hair even wilder than usual, her cheeks redder. Cabin fever had claimed her after all. Either that or she suffered from the same fever that was burning through him.

He needed to check Mrs. Thielsen's backyard to be sure no more strays—or any more serious intruder—had invaded D'Artagnan's territory. He needed to review his notes again, search for any small details that might pull the loose ends of the investigation together.

He knew his duty, but the fever dimmed duty, dimmed sense, and dimmed self-preservation. The fever wanted him to say to hell with the dogs, to hell with the case, to hell with the danger and offer to join her in the shower.

Fifteen minutes later, Daniel sat on the couch, flipping through the notebook he'd set on the coffee table and rubbing antiseptic cream into the long cat scratch across the back of his left hand. Between playing referee for Fleur and Edgar and D'Artagnan and rescuing damsels in distress, he looked as though he'd climbed a barbed wire fence to escape a secured facility. Tonight, he probably *belonged* in a secured facility, preferably a mental institution.

He closed the notebook. After reading all the facts of a case, trying to sort them into some kind of order, he'd normally set them aside and let his subconscious work while he listened to a little Dire Straits.

But tonight, his attention kept wandering to the sound of water running in the bathroom, to Destiny in the shower, the steam rising around her slim body . . . He growled and flipped the notebook open again.

The chime of the doorbell was a welcome distraction.

He shrugged his jacket on over his shoulder holster and moved to the door. Looking through the peephole, he saw Philip Brooks on his front step. Surprised, he opened the door.

"Hello, Daniel."

"Philip."

"May I come in?" Philip's thousand-watt smile had dimmed to about forty watts that evening.

"For a minute . . ." Daniel stepped aside, worry for Fiona overriding his desire to get rid of the man as quickly as possible. He no longer heard the shower running. "What brings you all the way out here tonight?"

"Fee. What else?" For the first time Daniel saw lines creasing Philip's fine, fair skin. "You know I don't like this investigation into Gage's death."

"You've made that clear."

"I suppose I have." Philip moved toward the couch. Daniel stepped forward to intercept him. This was not the evening for a long chat.

Philip frowned. "I can't really explain it. I know you're doing your job, but I don't think this is best for Fiona. It's as though . . . as though she *wants* Gage to have been murdered." He frowned, not satisfied with his own words. "She wants someone to blame. She seems in control, I know, but it's because she has this mission, to expose whoever is responsible for destroying her life."

He looked at Daniel. "Gage is dead, either way. In the end, she's going to have to face that. I'm afraid the longer she avoids it, the harder it's going to be."

"I understand your concern," Daniel said. "But this investigation isn't going to disappear. I don't have proof that Gage was murdered. I may never have it. But there are other crimes involved that have to be solved.

"Fiona's a brave woman. I know she's your little sister, but you can't protect her from life. She needs your support, not your interference."

Philip barked a humorless laugh. "Just what I knew you'd say. And you're right, I—"

"Daniel?" Destiny's voice came from the hall.

Daniel whirled to intercept her, but he was too late. She stepped into the living room wearing an old, ratty, terry cloth robe and huge fuzzy slippers, her wet hair corkscrewing down to her shoulders. She couldn't have looked sexier in a black silk negligee.

"I ran out of the toothpaste in my travel bag. Can I borrow—" She saw Philip, and her face paled, then flushed red. "Oh, I'm sor—I didn't hear—"

She looked to Daniel, panic in her eyes.

"You can use my toothpaste," he said, his gaze holding hers, cautioning her to stay calm. "I'll be there in a minute."

She understood, forcing a smile to her lips. "Thanks. Good evening, Mr. Brooks. Please excuse me. I'm sorry I'm not presentable."

"I apologize for barging in at this unconscionable hour," Philip said smoothly. "Good evening, Ms. Millbrook."

When she had retreated down the hall, he turned to Daniel, a rueful smile on his lips. "Well, there you go. I should have known when you refused to introduce us in the park, but I had to make an ass of myself dropping in on her at the library. But that's just the way my month has gone."

He reached into his pocket and pulled out a rolled-up packet of photocopies. "I won't keep you any longer. This is what I came by for. As Pleasance Geary's lawyer, it wasn't difficult for me to obtain a list of the principal ShopSmart investors. I thought you might have to fiddle around with warrants and figured I'd save you the trouble."

He handed Daniel the papers. "I don't know how much help they'll be, but if Gage *was* murdered, I do want whoever's responsible to be caught."

Daniel flipped through the sheets, scanning the names, some of which he hadn't seen before. "Thanks. This could be useful."

Philip shook his hand. "If there's anything else I can do, just ask. I promise not to grouse about it."

"Fiona will be okay, Philip."

"I know." He opened the door. Cool air flowed in, hinting at autumn. "Apologize to the lady for me again, please. I should have called first. You're a lucky man, Parks."

Daniel watched him walk to his car, watched the taillights disappear up the lane. He rubbed the back of his neck; it didn't ease the tension there.

He could have asked Philip not to mention seeing Destiny, but that would have required an explanation he'd rather not give. He didn't want Destiny connected to this case by anyone who didn't already know she was. And he hoped he could count on Philip's innate gallantry not to mention the incident to anyone.

But the memory of Tessa's offhand comment about Fiona offering to buy Philip a money clip like Barris Williams's sent ripples of apprehension up and down his spine.

He closed the door and leaned against it. This case was going to give him an ulcer.

The scent of floral shampoo floated to him on the steamy air from the bathroom, reminding him of Destiny's presence in his bedroom. In his bed.

This case was going to drive him to drink.

Chapter 10

When Destiny's eyes fluttered open the next morning, she realized the earthquake cracks in the ceiling of Daniel's bedroom had taken on a disturbing familiarity. The leaden weight on her legs, too, was familiar: Edgar, who'd taken to splitting the night between her bed and Daniel's futon. She no longer needed to fumble awkwardly to find the switch for the lamp on the bedside table.

Fleur whined again, and she remembered what had awakened her.

"You want to go out?"

The dog leaped to her feet, tail thumping wildly against the bed. Edgar bared his teeth in protest but had given up hissing. He wasn't going to embarrass himself by launching into a snit if Fleur wouldn't even notice.

Destiny glanced at the alarm clock on the table. Six-thirty.

The whine rose in intensity.

"Give it a rest, Fleur." But she dragged her feet out from under the cat and swung them into the cold morning air. Having been stuck here in Daniel's house for four days, she was going positively stir crazy, but it was worse for the dog. Fleur's energy level demanded a forty-five minute walk every day. It shouldn't be surprising that she was beginning to act out.

Destiny threw on jeans and her fuchsia sweatshirt—she didn't want to run into Daniel while wearing her nightshirt. Or maybe she did, but she wasn't going to think about that. She pulled on a pair of heavy socks and reached for her slippers. She paused, her gaze resting on her athletic shoes under the chair by the door.

Six-thirty.

She moved to the window and pulled aside the curtain. Thick fog swirled outside, the dawn light a glimmer in the grayness.

Thick fog on a cold, early Sunday morning. No one in his or her right mind would be out. Barris Williams wasn't due to return to Hope Point until that afternoon.

Daniel had mentioned there was a path down to Bright Cove Beach at the end of his lane.

Not giving herself time to think more about it, Destiny pulled on her shoes and clicked Fleur's leash to her collar. The dog jumped in delight, thudding against the door.

"Shh!" Destiny ordered, letting Fleur drag her down the hall. "If Daniel hears us, we're sunk."

She paused in the kitchen long enough to down a tall glass of orange juice and leave Daniel a note. Then they were out the front door and into the thick gray silence of the morning.

Fleur dashed forward in spurts, pausing after each lunge to sniff the secrets—and half the pollen—out of the weeds at the edge of the road. One such weed patch nearly hid the plain brown marker for the trailhead. Destiny unsnapped the leash, letting Fleur plunge into the undergrowth beneath the moss-hung spruces guarding the cliff edge.

The trail—if it could be called a trail—was probably impassible after a heavy rain. But Destiny hopped and slid her way toward the sound of the sea, refusing to think about how her thighs would ache on the return climb.

At the bottom, the trail disappeared, leaving her to find her own way over a pile of boulders to the sand. As she looked out across the slate-gray sea, she realized two things. She'd dropped beneath the fog layer and could see much farther than she'd expected. And she wasn't the only one crazy enough to be out on the beach at this hour on a Sunday morning.

Black forms, slick as seals in their wet suits, bobbed far out in the surf, meditating with the swell of the sea as they waited for the perfect wave. Destiny doubted they'd find it today, with the tide purring in under the windless fog. But she found herself glad to see the surfers, glad to be able to view strangers without feeling a shiver of threat.

Fleur had already found the water and ran back to Destiny, her yellow coat dripping a dark trail across the dry sand, her mouth open in a grin of delight.

"Stop! Shake!"

Fleur happily ignored the first command, bounding near before ridding herself of her load of seawater. Her eyes gleamed at Destiny's shriek. She danced backward, begging Destiny to play.

Destiny laughed. It didn't matter how foul a mood she was in or what pair of shoes Fleur had most recently destroyed; that grin got her every time.

"All right. Go find a stick, and I'll throw it. Stick! Get a stick!"

Fleur jumped and looked down between her paws to see if she had a stick she'd forgotten about. When she saw nothing, the suggestion clicked in, and she dashed toward the base of the cliff, where the highest summer tides had left a tangle of driftwood.

Destiny followed, ready to pick out her own throwing stick. Sometimes Fleur's idea of a good stick was a piece of kindling that splintered with one good chomp of her jaws, and sometimes she grabbed the better part of a tree.

"Hey! Ow!"

The loud cry of annoyance brought Destiny's gaze up from the sand. She heard a desperate scrabbling sound, then

Fleur reappeared from behind a boulder, her body posture somewhere between abject submission and hey-isn't-this-a-great-game. Behind her appeared a young man with a canvas slouch hat pulled low over his auburn hair, a scowl darkening his cold-reddened face.

"Are you all right?" Destiny asked, grabbing Fleur's collar.

"Other than almost killing myself—" He stopped, studying her. For a second his expression went slack. Then a crooked smile lit his face. "Destiny! Destiny Millbrook. We meet again."

Something twisted in her stomach. He looked familiar, sounded familiar, but . . .

"Jake. Jake Westing." He held out his hand. "I thought I made an unforgettable impression at the library the other day."

Her knees wobbled in relief. "Of course. The slacker."

"Ow." He put a hand over his heart. "Not exactly the impression I was aiming for."

"Sorry." She laughed at his injured expression. "I had to fend off your boss after you left the desk. Philip Brooks is your boss, right?"

"That's me, Jake Westing, underpaid legal aide."

"What are you doing out here in the cold and the fog on your day off? It is your day off, right?"

"Of course." He winked. "I'm checking out the cliff. I like to climb."

Destiny gazed upward at the dull caramel-colored sandstone. "That stuff's pretty loose. It could be dangerous."

"It's not too bad if you're careful. And I've got all my gear." He turned so she could see the backpack he carried. "As soon as I climb above dog level, I should be fine."

"I'm sorry Fleur bothered you."

161

"She just startled me. She's a nice-looking dog. Here, pooch."

Destiny let loose Fleur's collar. Fleur moved forward toward Jake's outstretched hand, then paused, her body tense. She looked back at Destiny, her tail drooping between her legs.

"It's okay," Destiny assured her.

But Fleur turned away, tail down, returning halfheartedly to her search for the perfect piece of driftwood.

"I must have scared her as much as she scared me," Jake apologized. "I almost landed on her when I slipped off the rocks."

Destiny cringed. "I really am sorry. You're sure you're all right?"

"Yeah, this is great." He turned the full force of his wide-eyed smile on her. "Showing off your climbing gear to a beautiful woman is at least as fulfilling as actually climbing."

He shifted his backpack, glancing at her from under the brim of his hat. "Look, you want to go get a cup of coffee or some breakfast? It must be nearly seven. I bet that little place in Shell Creek is open by now—it caters to fishermen."

He couldn't be asking her out. "I don't know that your girlfriend would appreciate it if I did."

"My girlfriend?"

"The eggplant parmigiana lady."

"Oh, right." He smiled crookedly. "That was a disaster. The recipe I found had pine nuts in it. How was I supposed to know she was allergic to pine nuts? Two hours in the emergency room is not the best way to start a relationship."

Destiny shook her head, biting back her laughter. "Oh, Jake."

He shrugged. "Probably just as well. I'm not much for long-distance romance. So, are you free? It's only breakfast.

You don't have to commit to dinner tonight until later."

He *was* asking her out. "Jake, how old are you?" Four or five years younger than she was, she'd guess.

"Now I'm shocked." He shook his head at her. "I never would have pictured you for an ageist."

"I'm not—"

"You're turning me down."

Something hard bumped against her hand. A solid length of wave-polished wood. She heaved it toward the sea. Fleur pounded after it, silent in the sand.

"It's not you, Jake," she said, wondering how she'd gotten herself into this—on a Sunday morning before she'd even showered, for heaven's sake. "I'm just . . . It's—"

"There's someone else."

And that was it. No matter that Daniel didn't want to be involved. She couldn't imagine dating another man while she felt this way about him. She wondered how long that would last. The thought depressed her. It felt as if it might last a very long time.

"There's someone else," she agreed.

He shrugged. "You can't blame a guy for trying. But if it doesn't work out with this other dude, you know where to find me."

"When there's not a mysterious stomach flu epidemic that only strikes legal aides."

"You really know how to hurt a guy when he's down."

Destiny had the feeling she hadn't crushed Jake's ego. "I'd better throw Fleur's stick before she scares somebody else. Take care, Jake."

"Yeah, you, too. I'll see you around."

Destiny wandered down to the water and attempted to retrieve Fleur's stick without getting wet—a hopeless task, but it amused Fleur to no end. Destiny heaved the stick into the surf, watching Fleur crash into the waves after it. In the arctic currents off the northern California coast a human without a wet suit would succumb to hypothermia in about twenty minutes. Fleur wanted to swim forever.

Destiny glanced back toward the cliff. Jake Westing had disappeared, continuing his search for a good climb. The relatively low sandstone cliffs at Bright Cove seemed an odd choice. Most climbers spent their time on the high rocks at Union Cove or around the other side of Cypress Head. Maybe he'd gotten bored with those.

She wandered up the beach, throwing Fleur's stick, looking for seashells. She wished she hadn't run into Jake Westing. For the past couple of days, she'd managed more or less successfully not to think about the future of her tenuous relationship with Daniel Parks.

She'd kept her distance; he'd kept his. She'd let herself simply enjoy his company, discussing the case, books, music, life. The night before she'd even started reading the copy of *The Godwulf Manuscript* he'd lent her. She'd needed something to distract her from thinking about being in Daniel's bed. And the book had hooked her; she'd read until almost midnight.

Spenser. She shook her head in disbelief.

She'd started thinking of Daniel as a real friend. Someone she could talk to about anything. Someone she could be herself around. Someone she could share toothpaste with and bake chocolate chip cookies for. She'd even fixed the leaky faucet in his kitchen.

And then Jake Westing had to ask her out.

A year ago she'd have fallen head over heels for a guy like Jake. Too cute a smile for his own good, totally irresponsible, happy-go-lucky. Utterly charming in his self-centered egoism.

But she'd discovered that a stable, thoughtful, down-to-earth man could be just as much fun to be with, could touch places in her heart and mind that no other man had touched—and he didn't want to compromise his duty by becoming involved. Responsibility as a personality trait had a definite downside to it.

Seeing Jake had reminded her that sooner or later this arrangement with Daniel would end. She'd go back to her house, back to her job, back to her life. Once there, she might never see him again.

The thought chilled her.

She reached for Fleur's stick, discovering that her fingers were so numb she could hardly feel the wood. Maybe it wasn't only her thoughts chilling her after all.

Seawater soaked the lower half of her jeans and the shoes she'd forgotten to take off. Looking around, she realized the fog had crept lower, wrapping cold, damp tendrils through her hair, working the chill down into her sweatshirt, and hiding the surfers from view.

In fact, the surfers were probably long gone. Surely they had given up waiting for a decent wave and had headed home for a huge breakfast and a double espresso.

Come to think of it, breakfast didn't sound like such a bad idea. Destiny glanced at her watch. Seven-thirty. Daniel was going to kill her.

She shouldn't have put it that way. Glancing around, her eye caught on shifting drifts of fog, ghostly movement that sent a shiver up her spine.

She felt exposed, the only spark of color on the dun and gray beach, the only living creature. She couldn't see Fleur, couldn't even hear the jingling of her tags, only the shush of the sea.

She opened her mouth to call, but no words came. The silence choked back the sound that would mark her, expose her even more.

Then she heard the splash of feet hitting the water, saw the white flash of Fleur's teeth as the big dog loped toward her, stopping a yard away to rest and pant.

"Good girl. What a good girl you are."

Fleur's tail waved in acknowledgment.

"Had enough? It's time to go back."

A crease appeared between the dog's eyes, and her tail began to droop.

"Don't give me that. You're tired, too. Let's get some breakfast, okay? Breakfast?"

Fleur's tail perked up. She began to trot back the way they had come, and Destiny followed, shrugging off the irrational panic that had gripped her. Fleur's tail waving in front of her, the squish of her wet shoes, the cry of a distant seagull—all felt soothingly familiar. But she couldn't dismiss the feeling of danger lurking in the obscuring fog.

"It's all Daniel's fault," she muttered to herself, letting her doubts turn to annoyance. "How long does he think we can stay locked up here, Fleur? I'm about bored enough to chase Edgar around myself. I've missed three days of work, two softball practices, the game yesterday, and, at this rate, I'm going to miss the tournament next weekend. I don't even want to think about Serena coaching those games."

Her voice faded as her pace flagged in the deep, dry sand above the rising tide. The harder she worked, the slower she seemed to move. Her heart thudded in her chest from the effort, reminding her unpleasantly of the physical effects of fear.

"Fleur, wait for me."

Unexpectedly, Fleur turned back to her, matching her pace to Destiny's, her head up, her tail no longer waving.

Destiny stopped, a metallic taste in her mouth.

The fog and the low-level white noise of the sea effectively sucked all other sound from the landscape. She heard nothing, saw nothing to cause either her own trepidation or Fleur's sudden nervousness.

They'd reached the spot where she thought the path up to Daniel's lane began, but dread altered her perspective, changing the shapes of the boulders as fog obscured the top of the cliff.

Fleur moved forward, clambering over the rocks. Destiny followed. And, of course, there was the path, right where it was supposed to be.

Destiny allowed herself a smile of relief.

"Good thing *you* remembered the way, Fleur."

But Fleur had stopped, frozen, at the first turn of the switchback path, the fur on her neck bristling.

Destiny's relief disappeared. "What is it?"

Fleur glanced back, her expression troubled. But she moved forward again, her fur slowly lying down, her nose returning to its hunt for exciting smells.

Destiny shut her eyes briefly, reminding herself that the first time Fleur had seen a snowman she'd succumbed to hysterics. The dog was still leery of the bizarre white creatures, passing them in stiff-legged suspicion.

Fleur's odd behavior probably came from the strangeness of the past few days—a new house, new housemates, not getting as much exercise as she was accustomed to. Destiny remembered that Fleur had also acted strangely when Jake Westing had tried calling her to him. Fleur generally assumed that every outstretched hand held a dog biscuit.

Her refusal to make friends with Jake was a strong sign that her current behavior stemmed from nothing more serious than an uneasy mood.

Of course, it was possible that Jake had tumbled on top of her or even swung a kick in her direction when Fleur surprised him. Though the Lab hadn't seemed upset when she'd dashed from behind the rocks. For a moment she'd tried to tug her collar out of Destiny's grip to go see if she couldn't convince Jake to holler again.

Fleur hadn't started acting strangely until Destiny had released her and she'd moved close enough to Jake to smell him . . .

"Fleur, wait." She had a sudden, sick feeling in her stomach.

What if Fleur had smelled something she didn't like on the trail? What if it was Jake?

Nothing strange about his using this trail. He'd been looking for places to climb. He might have found this trail and decided to see where it led.

Fleur's cold nose pushed against her hand, followed by a small, subdued whine.

Fleur always whined when Destiny stopped on a walk. Yet it seemed different this time. Just her own attack of nerves, undoubtedly, but Fleur sounded more anxious than eager.

What had Jake really been doing at the beach this morning? Even as a non-climber, she knew this wasn't the best place for rock climbing. Had he actually carried any climbing equipment in his backpack? And if he had, why choose to do his climbing here? Why choose a spot that would lead the climber up into the backyards of private homes?

If Jake had succeeded in scaling the cliff where she and Fleur had found him, he would have ended up very close to Daniel's backyard.

What if she'd upset him more than she thought when she'd turned down his offer of breakfast? No. She couldn't picture Jake as the type to turn into a stalker after a rejection. She doubted she'd even wounded his ego. He didn't seem to care that much.

That insight didn't improve her mood. Words like *sociopath* came to mind. The chill pooling in her stomach had nothing to do with the numbness of her hands and feet.

This is ridiculous. If Jake had been looking for her, if he'd wanted to hurt her, he could have done so down on the beach. *In front of the surfers?*

Fleur whined again, her ears pricking forward, her muscles tensing. Over the sound of her own labored breathing, Destiny caught a hint of the noise that had alerted her dog. Something rustling against scrub and beach grass. The scrape of a shoe seeking footing on slick clay dirt.

Someone was climbing down the path toward her.

Saplings, the fog, the turns in the path, all hid him from her view, but even now he might be able to see her, a splash of eye-catching color in her fuchsia sweatshirt.

Feeling like an idiot but unable to quiet the pounding of her heart, Destiny turned and skidded back down the path. Fleur pushed close against her, the dog's hackles raised again. A low growl began deep in Fleur's throat.

"Shh!" Destiny ordered, her own breath harsh with panic. She scrambled over the boulders, turning to look behind her.

Fleur hadn't followed. The dog remained in the middle of the path, looking up the cliff, her legs planted stiffly, head lowered.

"Fleur!" She hardly dared whisper, but Fleur heard and glanced at her. "Fleur, come!"

But the dog looked away, staring in the direction from which her pursuer came. Louder and closer.

"Fleur!" Destiny's voice broke on the name. Her limbs shook, barely able to hold her to the rocks. She could feel again the hands on her neck in the park, choking her. She

could hear the sound of gunfire as her car spun out of control on the highway.

Whatever logic might tell her, her gut believed that Jake Westing had not come to this beach by accident and that he meant her harm. Never mind that he couldn't possibly know she was staying with Daniel.

But she couldn't leave Fleur.

With a sob, she dropped to the hard sand at the bottom of the path, scrabbling on hands and knees until she found a loose stone. It fit her hand like a baseball.

She rose unsteadily to her feet, praying her arm wasn't too limp to throw it. Of course, if he had a gun, the problem was moot.

Without warning Fleur launched herself forward. A vicious alarm tore from her throat, shredding the fog-heavy silence.

Destiny yelled, too, a primal sound that propelled her leaden feet forward. Suddenly in control of her muscles once more, she launched her rock upward as a warning, stooping in the next motion to grab another stone.

She heard rock hitting rock, a shout, heard Fleur's barking turn to panic.

"Destiny!" The roar stopped her with the force of a blow.

"Daniel?" His name came out in a croak.

Fleur flew around the corner of the trail, her ears back, tail down, eyes wild. She nearly knocked Destiny to the ground, then turned, feet spraying sand, and dashed past her again, back up the trail.

"Fleur?" Daniel's voice again. "Damn dog!"

And Fleur bounded back to Destiny, spinning on her butt at the bottom of the trail, turning to thunder up again.

"You scared her," Destiny called, her voice sounding strange in her ears. "She needs to run it off."

"I scared *her?*" And there he was, turning the corner, sliding down the last steep slope to where she stood. "I thought she was going to rip my throat out until she tried to lick my face."

Destiny was still attempting to swallow her own fear. "She didn't know it was you. She's never done that before. Maybe she's feeling overprotective after the attack in the park. She thought you were going to hurt me."

"Then she wasn't far wrong." On the slope, he loomed over her, his hair wild from sleep, his face creased with grim lines. "What the hell did you think you were doing, leaving the house like that? Can't I even sleep until seven on a Sunday morning without worrying you'll do something stupid?"

"I guess not." The stone slipped from her numb hand. "I'm sorry."

With one hand he gripped her shoulder; the other tilted her chin so she looked up into his face. "Do you have any idea how I felt, finding that note? I didn't know what time you'd left it, how long you'd been gone. I couldn't even see down to the beach."

"I'm sorry," she said again, caught between guilt and defiance. "I forgot I'm not supposed to have a life."

He opened his mouth to reply, then closed it again, his eyes as dark as the fog-shrouded sea as they bored into hers. "If anything had happened to you . . ."

She wiped a shaky hand across her eyes. "I know. I won't do it again. The last thing I want is to mess up your case."

His curse startled her. "Screw the case." The hand gripping her shoulder tightened convulsively. "Don't you have any idea . . . No, of course you don't."

His mouth covered hers, without a softening of his grimness, without reservation. She caught the reflection of her surprise in his eyes before hers closed and she leaned into him, giving in to the relief, wrapping her arms under his heavy field coat.

His hands cupped her face, guiding her closer, his mouth brushing her forehead, nose, cheeks, chin, before returning to her lips. Warmth flowed into her, out of her, washing away the chill of seawater, fog, and fear.

She opened her mouth, needing more of him, and his tongue found hers. She heard the sounds of desire in the back of her throat, heard the warning in her head that reminded her he didn't want to become involved. But she could only kiss him as fiercely as he kissed her, all the heat and confusion and intensity of her response burning from her mouth to his and back again.

She knew his taste, the way their breath mingled between them. She knew his scent, the warm, male mixture of sweat and soap and aftershave. She knew the feel of his ribs beneath her hands, the heat of his touch as his palms ran down her back.

She stepped into him, into his warmth. She could feel the evidence of his desire against her. Instead of pushing her away, he pulled her closer, his groan catching in her throat, melting through her body.

She pulled his shirt from the waistband of his pants. She ran her hands up underneath it, along the warm, hard muscles of his stomach. . . .

He jumped.

The sudden movement on the slick slope undid his balance, and they dropped in a tangle of flailing limbs. She landed hard on his chest, heard his sharp intake of breath. She tried to roll off him, but he pulled her to him tightly. Laughter softened the lines around his mouth.

"Your hands are cold."

"Not *that* cold."

"Like ice," he assured her.

"I got a little chilly throwing Fleur's stick, but in the past few minutes I've warmed up quite a bit." She stopped, unsure of how he'd respond.

"Obviously not enough." He wrapped her hands in his and pulled them up toward his face, stretching her more closely along his body. His breath blew warm on her fingers as he rubbed them between his palms.

She felt his heart beating against hers, felt heat soaking through her sweatshirt, through her jeans. His gaze locked with hers, and she couldn't move, couldn't breathe. His eyes, as dark and blue as the sea, never left hers as he raised her fingers to his lips and took them one by one into his mouth.

Electricity jumped in a surge from her fingertips to the pit of her stomach, and she knew he could see it in her eyes. Just as she could see the need that burned in his.

"I thought you said this was a bad idea," she managed to say, common sense still trying to warn her away.

"Actually, you said it was a bad idea, and I agreed with you." He stopped, the amusement fading from his eyes. "It was a bad idea. It's still a bad idea. But that doesn't mean it's not happening. I lost my objectivity a long time ago, Destiny. I can't continue pretending otherwise, and it would hardly be convincing if I tried at this point."

She couldn't deny that, since if she stretched herself, just so, she could feel the reaction in his body, see it in his eyes.

He touched her cheek and drew her down for a kiss, a gentle one this time, and then he let her go. "I owe you an apology."

For a moment her heart stopped. "Daniel, don't—"

"For reacting so strongly to your walk on the beach. I know the past few days haven't been easy on you. A short walk this early on a Sunday morning is something I might even have agreed to—with me along. It was just waking up to find you gone . . ."

"I shouldn't have left the house without asking you."

"True." He sat up, bringing her with him, his arm tightening around her shoulder. He almost smiled. "I kept imagining a skulking assassin—who looked strangely like Lars Holmgren, by the way—lurking behind every sand dune or pile of driftwood, just waiting for you to walk by. He was wearing a knit sailor's cap to hide the bandage where you'd conked him with the baseball bat."

Destiny's cheeks reddened. "I had something similar in mind when I threw that rock at you."

"Good thing you're not a better aim."

"I have very good aim, thank you," Destiny informed him, sitting up straighter. "I couldn't see you. It was meant to throw you off-balance so you couldn't hurt Fleur."

"I don't think Fleur needed any help. I never noticed how big her teeth were before." He shuddered. "Does she often attack innocent bystanders like that?"

"Of course not." Destiny frowned at him. "She's a well-behaved, gentle, friendly dog, or I wouldn't let her off her leash." The memory of those panic-filled moments filtered back into her mind, chilling away some of the warmth she'd regained. "She's never done anything like that before."

She looked at Daniel, trying to pinpoint why her unease had returned. "We did meet someone on the beach, someone I know from the library. Fleur didn't like him. I thought maybe he'd climbed this path and that was why she was so upset."

The relaxed warmth disappeared from Daniel's body. Without apparent haste or panic, he had them standing almost immediately, his gaze piercing the fog surrounding them.

"Do you know this man well?"

Destiny shook her head. "No, but he's just a feckless kid, really. I'm sure he's harmless."

Daniel raised an eyebrow at her. "Harmless enough that you'd throw a sizeable rock at his head?"

"I panicked."

"You're not the panicky type, Millbrook." He stuck his hand inside his coat, and she knew he was checking for his gun. "What about him made you nervous? Can you think of anything that might connect him to Gage Barclay? To Barris Williams?"

"No, or I'd have panicked sooner," she said, embarrassed by her earlier fear. "He was rock climbing. I suspect he's not particularly reliable—he skipped work the other day—but he seems nice enough. He works in your friend Philip Brooks's law firm."

The lines around Daniel's mouth hardened again. "Something made you suspicious of him, Destiny. What was it?"

His earlier words, half-joking, returned to her. "It sounds funny, but . . . he did wear a hat. He was wearing a baseball cap the other day, and he wore a ratty old hat today. It didn't bother me at the time. But there isn't any sun."

And something else troubled her, something that had been creeping up in the back of her mind for several minutes. She couldn't quite grasp it, but she could feel apprehension pushing again at the edges of her consciousness.

Daniel nodded, frowning up the trail. "And Fleur didn't like him."

Dread exploded full-blown into her brain. "Fleur! Daniel, where's Fleur?"

Chapter 11

"She's gone!"

Daniel heard the panic in Destiny's voice but kept his calm. "She can't be far. She was here just a second ago."

"No. It's been too long. She always comes back to check on me every couple of minutes."

"Always?" he asked, even as his senses strained for some indication of what might be happening out of sight in the fog. "She's probably chasing a rabbit or has found something irresistibly disgusting to roll in. She'll be fine until we have to turn the hose on her."

She frowned at him. "Fleur never rolls in anything disgusting."

"Mmm."

"Hardly ever." She tried to smile, but failed. "This really isn't like her, Daniel."

He heard her sharp intake of breath and grabbed her arm. "Don't call her."

Her dark eyes met his accusingly. "I thought you said there was nothing to worry about."

"I'm sure Fleur is fine." He met her gaze, decided there was no point in lying. "I'm just not willing to bet your safety on it."

She waited a long moment before responding. "You really think that someone—that Jake Westing—might be waiting for us up at your house."

"Probably not. Even if this guy Westing is the one who tried to strangle you in the park, you blew his plan by running into him on the beach. He'll be off somewhere weighing his options. Or, if he suspects you suspect him, hightailing it out of the area."

Which, all things considered, Daniel could live with. Once a hired gun's cover was blown, he rarely returned to finish the job.

And that's all this Jake Westing person could be—a hired killer. No green law clerk would have any reason to want Gage Barclay dead. Which left the second most immediate question unresolved: Who wanted Gage—and now Destiny—dead badly enough to hire someone to kill them? Barris Williams? Pleasance Geary?

Or someone with a tie to Jake the clerk? Someone with his career as invested in the ShopSmart project as Williams's was? Someone who'd tried to convince Daniel to drop the investigation. Someone who'd seen Destiny in Daniel's house just the evening before.

Daniel didn't even want to think it.

And right now he couldn't. Because the most immediate question facing him at the moment was the whereabouts of the hired killer.

"We'll go up the beach to the north end. We can walk to the gas station in Shell Creek and call for reinforcements." He glanced at the boulders they'd have to climb over to get to the beach. He didn't want to send Destiny over first, but neither did he want to leave her waiting here.

"What about Fleur?"

He'd send Destiny first and stay close behind her. "I don't like leaving her any more than you do, but she knows where my house is. She'll find her way back eventually."

"I'm not leaving her behind."

"Destiny, this is not negotiable. She's—"

"Don't you tell me she's just a dog." Her eyes glittered with angry tears, her hands clenching. "She was willing to risk her life for me earlier. She'd never desert me. Besides, I

177

think your plan is stupid."

"That's a mature argument."

Her hands unclenched, disarmed by his response. "What I mean is, what if Jake did plan to wait for me on this path? If he saw you come down here and heard all our shouting, wouldn't he be just as likely to guess our plan and wait for us at the other end of the beach as to stick around at your house?"

"No." He met her tight-lipped glare with one of his own. "But it's remotely possible. Here." He shrugged out of his khaki field coat and handed it to her. "Put this on and button up the collar. Next time you sneak out of a safe house, you might choose a different color sweatshirt."

She did as he asked, a small miracle. He helped her with the buttons; her fingers still felt icy to his touch.

"All right. Stay down here in the boulders, out of sight. If Fleur comes back, keep her with you. You have her leash?"

Destiny nodded.

"Good. How about your watch? Okay. If you hear anyone coming down this trail or if I don't come back in twenty minutes, I want you to get up the beach and to the gas station as fast as you can. Understand?"

"But—"

"With or without Fleur or me. Our lives might depend on it. Got it?"

"Daniel . . ."

He could see the fine bones beneath the skin of her face. The vulnerability in her eyes pulled at his heart.

"Please . . . be careful," she pleaded.

As long as he'd thrown his objectivity out the window . . . He caught her face with his hands and kissed her, savoring the soft sweetness of her lips.

"I will."

"Promise."

"I'll be back." He smiled at her. "I'm not intimidated by your independence. Check your watch."

While she glanced at her wrist, he slipped away, up the trail, past the rocks, through the tangle of brush and vines. He pushed aside his fear for Destiny, pushed aside the memory of holding her to him, and focused his senses on the environment around him, letting his ears and eyes absorb his surroundings and filter them for anything that didn't fit.

He saw gouges in the sandy dirt where Fleur had bounded up the path. He heard a crow call in the trees at the top of the cliff.

He'd checked his gun before charging out his front door that morning. That seemed an age ago. He paused near the top of the trail to check it one more time. Fully loaded. Ready.

In all his years on the Hope Point police force, he'd never had to use his gun. But he was never unprepared to use it.

A line of cedars and Sitka spruce offered cover as he slipped behind the houses across the street from his. Moving quickly, he crossed the street farther down and ran back in the same direction, stopping at the Thielsens' side door, safely out of sight of his own house. If anyone was watching for him, he wasn't going to be an easy target.

He surprised Mrs. Thielsen in her old orange bathrobe, but she let him use her phone.

He drilled it into the heads of rookie officers that it was better to call for backup to rescue a treed cat than to forget to call when help was really needed. Kermit would never let him live it down if he got himself shot playing Dirty Harry.

Shell Creek fell under the county sheriff's jurisdiction, and it turned out the nearest deputies were on another call. He called the Hope Point Police Department for Kermit, but even with all reasonable speed, it would take the squad car at least ten minutes to reach his house. In the meantime, he might as well assess the situation.

He slipped out the side door after asking Mrs. Thielsen to keep D'Artagnan inside until he returned. He followed the fence between his yard and Mrs. Thielsen's until he reached the cliff's edge.

Over the sound of the surf far below, he heard the muffled noise of frantic barking from the other side of the fence. Fleur. A weight lifted off his heart. He found a warped board in the fence that allowed him to peer through to his house.

The yard was empty of intruders. What held his gaze was Fleur's rear end sticking high in the air, one front leg, both back legs, and her tail flailing, the rest of her somehow forced through the cat door into the kitchen.

Daniel closed his eyes and counted to ten.

Destiny lasted eight minutes. She figured Daniel knew her well enough by this time that if he really thought there was serious danger, he would have tied her to a rock before leaving her.

He played everything by the book. She could respect that. But she couldn't sit there doing nothing when Fleur might have fallen off the cliff or been hit by a car . . . or been knifed by a frustrated Jake Westing.

So after eight minutes that lasted so long she became convinced her watch must have malfunctioned, she started up the trail. Her feet were still numb with cold, but by the time she scrambled to the top of the cliff, the rest of her felt flushed with heat.

She paused to catch her breath, and as her breathing softened, she heard barking from Daniel's house, fifty feet away.

She bit her lip to keep from crying out in relief. He'd found her. Daniel had found Fleur and locked her in the house before coming back to get her.

Legs shaky, she trotted toward the house. He'd yell at her for not waiting, but she had to see him, had to see Fleur, had to know they were okay. She opened her mouth to call Daniel's name, but the word never reached her lips. A gunshot fractured the morning silence into a hundred thousand mind-splitting shards.

When Daniel finished his ten-count, the scene hadn't changed. Fleur's barking sounded ragged, as though she'd worn her throat hoarse in her frenzy. He pictured Edgar sitting on a kitchen chair just out of reach, taunting the dog.

He swung himself around the end of the fence, into his yard.

"Fleur! What were you thinking?"

At the sound of his voice, the Lab's bark changed, and the scrabbling legs abruptly reversed. She popped free of the cat door with a speed that flipped her over onto her back. For a moment she was nothing but a writhing tangle of legs and whipcord spine.

She turned to grab something from the doorstep before trotting toward him, eyes anxious, limping awkwardly on one front leg.

"Don't tell me you dislocated your shoulder." He knelt down as she neared him. "Serves you right, fool dog."

He had in his head the sequence of events that would follow. He'd scratch her ears, lead her to the house, unlock the back door, shut her in the bedroom—away from Edgar—before calling off Kermit and returning to Destiny.

He would have been dead before he reached the back door.

As Fleur neared him, pushing herself on her bad leg, he saw what she carried in her mouth: a ragged scrap of denim.

In an instant of clarity he knew what she'd been after through the cat door. What had taunted her. It wasn't Edgar.

Time stopped. He knelt in the middle of his large, treeless backyard. He'd never reach the fence. Never reach the wall of the house. He'd die there, behind his own home before the Hope Point squad car arrived. Nothing would prevent the killer from stalking down to the beach and shooting Destiny.

Daniel threw himself forward with desperate power.

Daniel heard his kitchen window exploding, felt fire sting the top of his shoulder. He stumbled to his outdoor picnic table, and heaved it onto its side.

Another shot. The bullet tore the heavy redwood like cardboard, leaving a ragged hole inches from his head. A hand gun, his mind assessed the sound and effect of the shooter's weapon. A big one. Better for close work than the rifle the man had used before.

Pistol in his hand, Daniel fired back. He had no way of positioning himself for a good shot, but he knew that return fire would make anyone nervous. The killer's next bullet went wild.

But that wouldn't last long.

It was only a matter of time—minutes, seconds—before the man in his house began a systematic pattern of fire across the sideways tabletop. Only a matter of time before a bullet struck something vital.

Daniel's best hope was a break for the house. He doubted he'd be so lucky as to get just another crease on his shoulder.

He bunched his legs to spring. One . . . two . . .

Glass shattered, the sound more surprising than another gunshot. A window. Someone had thrown something through one of the windows on the side of his house.

Daniel didn't have to guess who. And he didn't have time to be angry that she'd ignored his directions once again.

He heaved himself forward, around the end of the table. His feet slipped in the wet grass as he ran, and he fell once, but his momentum carried him on a roll up to the wall of the house beneath the kitchen window.

He heard gunfire out the other window, heard loud, frantic cursing when the gunman turned back to the yard uncertain whether Daniel remained behind the table or not.

He shifted himself to a sitting position, surprised to see blood oozing from slits in his shirt. He'd rolled into the broken glass from the window the gunman had shot out. He patted his arms and legs and decided he hadn't cut anything crucial.

Daniel assessed his new situation. Definitely an improvement over the picnic table. In fact, given the status quo, he could probably sit tight here until Kermit arrived with reinforcements.

But, of course, the status refused to quo.

The gunman fired again, but not at the table. A divot of dirt and grass popped up beside Fleur as the dog tried to limp toward Daniel.

Daniel focused on the smooth, shining, *expensive* panes of glass filling his floor-to-ceiling living room windows. Shielding his eyes, he fired at one, distracting the killer from the dog.

He kicked out the rest of the pane with his shoe. A shot buzzed past through the empty window frame, but Daniel guessed the gunman had taken cover behind the kitchen counter, which would reduce his line of sight into the living room.

As Daniel peeked cautiously around the edge of the window frame, just far enough to gauge the possibilities the living room offered for cover, he saw movement across the room. The front doorknob had turned, and a crack of light appeared along the doorframe. No one in his or her right mind would . . .

Destiny would. He cursed again.

Destiny slipped through the front door, the echo of gun-shots ringing in her ears. With the short hall leading to the kitchen, Jake probably couldn't see the front door. But if he'd heard the door open . . .

The world exploded again into a burst of gunfire. She dove forward, landing against the doorway between the hall and the kitchen. It took her several seconds to realize no one was shooting at her.

From her position she could see puffs of stuffing erupting from the couch in the living room, hear bullets splintering the coffee table. Daniel was crouched behind his easy chair, re-turning fire at someone she couldn't see. Blood streaked his shirt, and she thought she saw the slash of a wound along the side of his head.

Her vision dimmed in panic, and she leaned back against the wall, fighting for self-control until she achieved it.

She pushed herself to her feet. Ringing, exploding noise once more covered any sounds she made. Hefting her re-maining rock, she spun around the doorway into the kitchen.

Jake Westing crouched behind the counter that separated the living room from the kitchen area, his pistol in his left hand, firing around the edge of the counter at Daniel.

Her movement—or instinct—turned Jake's head as she came through the doorway. His eyes widened in surprise, but there was no hesitation as he swung toward her, his pistol smacking against the counter as he brought it around.

She didn't have time for fear to spoil her aim. The rock left her hand true. Jake had no chance to dodge. The rock hit him squarely in the forehead, sending him sprawling to the tiles.

Daniel reached him before Jake even hit the floor, retrieving the gun that dropped limply from his hand, rolling him onto his stomach to tie his hands with his own belt.

Jake groaned and shifted. Destiny dropped beside him, grabbing her rock, ready to strike him again. But when Daniel rolled him onto his back, she saw that it wouldn't be necessary. Jake's eyes rolled loosely in their sockets, the skin on his forehead already beginning to bruise where the stone had struck him.

Even knowing he'd tried to kill her and Daniel, even having seen the gun in his hand, the willingness to shoot her in his eyes, she still thought he looked like a harmless kid lying there on the kitchen floor.

Daniel sank to the tiles, leaning his head back against the cupboards. "Nice throw."

"He's not going to die, is he?" Destiny asked, disturbed by Jake's pallor and the shallowness of his breathing.

"No, but I don't mind if you keep trying." Daniel reached out to turn Jake's head. He'd lost his hat during the gunfight, and in his thick ruddy hair Destiny saw a white gauze bandage.

"From my baseball bat."

Daniel nodded.

Destiny thought she might be sick. But then she looked back at Daniel and saw the blood again, and all thought of Jake Westing left her.

"You're hurt!" She scooted around Jake and gingerly touched Daniel's shirt. "I'm going to call an ambulance."

"No." He grabbed her wrist, preventing her from rising. "It's not that bad."

"You're bleeding."

"Not anymore, I don't think." He touched his shoulder and looked down at his chest to make sure. "Just a couple of cuts. No bullet wounds."

With her free hand, she touched his temple. Blood oozed from what looked like a rug burn there. "What about this one?"

He winced as she dabbed at it with a tissue from her pocket. "Maybe he winged me when I was diving for the armchair."

Destiny frowned at him. "What were you thinking? Bullets can't penetrate furniture? He had the high ground here in the kitchen."

Daniel looked at her, one eyebrow cocked. "I had to do something to distract him from your dramatic entrance. If I'd known you were going to attack an armed man with nothing but a rock . . ." He paused. "I guess I should have known, at that."

She began unbuttoning his shirt. "I'm sorry. I know you had everything under control."

He batted at her hands. "I didn't say I wasn't grateful. That first rock you threw saved my life."

She met his gaze, not knowing how to share the terror that had gripped her at the thought of losing him. "And you saved mine. It's my fault you got shot at in the first place, looking for Fleur."

"That's all right. She saved my life, too. She showed me that Westing was hiding in here."

Destiny had been trying not to wonder, not to think of Jake's shooting at Fleur. Now that she had, she couldn't breathe. "Daniel?"

He caught her hands and pulled them away from his shirt. "It's okay. Fleur's going to be okay, just like I'm going to be okay. I think she's dislocated her shoulder, but he didn't hit her."

As if in response to his words, an anxious whine sounded

Dangerous Moonlight

from the shattered living room window.

"Fleur?" Destiny leaned around the end of the counter to see her dog hobble over the low, jagged sill, the Lab's thick otter tail beginning to wag low and fast at the sight of Destiny's face. "Come here, baby."

Daniel released one hand, and she held it out to Fleur. The dog glanced warily at Jake, then edged to Destiny and Daniel, licking Destiny's outstretched hand, then wiggling closer to lick Daniel's face.

"Ugh!" He pushed at her muzzle, and the Lab pressed forward even more eagerly, happy to see him playing. "Fleur! Aagh! Dog lips touched my lips!"

Laughter unstrung Destiny's muscles, and she sagged beside Daniel, leaning against him and the cupboard. "Fleur, down. Down!"

With a ragged sigh, Fleur eased herself to the ground, leaning away from her injured leg. Daniel's hand rested on her head, pushing back her ears as he looked into her eyes. "Good dog. You're a good dog, Fleur. Thank you."

She thumped her tail in response and eased her jaw up onto Daniel's thigh, her eyes flicking from his to Destiny's and back.

"That's right," Destiny said approvingly. "You hold him down. I'm going to check his wounds."

"I'm fine."

"You don't look fine."

"Well . . ." He looked at her. "I do have one place that hurts."

"Where?"

He lifted a finger to his lower lip. "Right here. Hurts like hell. Maybe you could make it feel better?"

She punched his shoulder.

"Hey! Is that any way to treat someone who's been shot?"

And then she kissed him. Hard. And he kissed her back. Fear and anger and shyness disappeared in the warmth of his touch, and her heart felt as though it might expand right through her rib cage. The rest of the world faded away.

She felt as if she could spend the rest of her life right there in his arms, regardless of the blood seeping onto his field coat, of the cold air pouring through broken windows, of Jake Westing moaning beside them, of the sirens splitting the morning air, of the shouts ringing outside the house . . .

Chapter 12

The loud clearing of Kermit Riggs's throat brought Daniel back to the present with an unpleasant snap.

"Sorry to interrupt," Kermit said, not sounding sorry at all. "Some of the neighbors heard gunshots. We like to check out that sort of thing."

Daniel glared up at the lanky young officer. "Took you long enough to get here."

"You didn't say you were going to engage in a gun battle with a desperate criminal by yourself."

"Don't look at me. Fleur decided to play Rambo."

Fleur looked up at Kermit with adoration and thumped her tail but didn't try to rise.

"Is she all right?" Kermit knelt to take an anxious look at the dog.

"Why, thank you, Kerry, I'm fine," Daniel drawled as he rose and helped Destiny to her feet. "Just a few bullet wounds. All in the line of duty."

"She's hyperextended her leg or something," Kermit said, ignoring the sarcasm.

"Got it stuck in the cat door," Daniel explained.

"And her foot's cut."

"The glass." Daniel glanced around his kitchen. Window glass lay everywhere in shards and tiny glimmers. Bullet holes showed as bright splinters against the dark varnish of his cupboards. "I wonder if my homeowner's insurance covers shoot-outs."

"I think your microwave gave its life to the cause," Destiny said, looking dazed as she surveyed the damage.

"Don't even look at the living room," Kermit advised after a quick glance around the counter. He pushed himself to his feet. "I called an ambulance when I heard about the gunshots. I'm sure the paramedics can immobilize Fleur's leg until you can get her to the vet."

"Aaaah." The loud groan swung their attention to the other figure lying on the floor. "My head."

"That the perp?" Kermit asked.

Daniel nodded, pointing to the gun on the counter. "That's his."

"I'll have Martinez help me escort this guy to the squad car. She's checking the perimeter." He took a closer look at Daniel. "Why don't you sit down? You don't look so great."

"Thanks, Kerry."

"No problem, sir."

And then Kermit was gone. Almost gone. It took him a minute to disentangle his foot from the destroyed microwave's cord.

Destiny looked up at Daniel and opened her mouth.

"I'm fine," he insisted.

She gave him that skeptical look that made him want to kiss her. In fact, now that he *had* kissed her, he didn't think it would take much of anything to make him want to do it again.

"You practically collapsed after you tied Jake up," she reminded him.

He wasn't about to tell her that his legs had sagged in relief that Jake hadn't shot her. If he thought about how close she had come to being killed, he would have to sit down again.

She reached for his shirt. "At least let me take a look at the cuts on your chest."

He brushed her hands aside. "The paramedics will take care of it. I don't have time to be coddled right now. This isn't over yet."

Not until she stepped away from him, her arms crossed over her stomach, did he remember that the case, his job, had been his excuse for not becoming involved with her. *Reason.* Not excuse. And it must still be a valid reason; he just couldn't think why.

"Destiny—"

"No, it's all right. I understand." She tilted her chin up, her eyes narrowed. "You can't do your duty properly if you're distracted. You do what's necessary to wrap this up."

As clearly as if she'd said it, he heard the end of the challenge. *And then we'll see what happens.* Remembering her pain when she'd talked about her former boyfriend—what *was* his name?—he was struck by her courage.

And he knew he loved that about her. He loved her. Sensible or not. Unfinished case or not. And in the face of her courage, he could do no less than tell her—

"Morning, Detective." Officer Grace Martinez entered the kitchen with her usual impression of compact efficiency, Kermit on her heels like an ungainly Great Dane. She looked down at Jake Westing with displeasure. "This the loser we're transporting?"

Daniel saw Westing's eyes focus on Grace's strongly handsome features, her bobbed dark hair.

"You're breaking my heart," Westing said with an attempt at charm that left Daniel wanting to kick him.

"Can't hurt as bad as your broken head," Grace said without sympathy. "Get up."

She and Kermit heaved Jake to his feet over his complaints and escorted him to the door. Seeing the look on Destiny's face, Daniel was glad Westing was still too out of it to throw any comments her way. He would have had to shoot him.

When Destiny turned to him, he said, "I need to get down to the station, fill my lieutenant and the chief in on what's happening. I also want to see that Westing doesn't have a chance to talk with Barris Williams before I do." *Or with Philip Brooks,* he added to himself. What it would do to Fiona if . . . He couldn't think about it.

They heard another siren approaching. The ambulance.

"Fleur?" Destiny asked.

"I'll drop you off at the vet, whichever clinic has emergency duty this weekend. You can call the station when you're finished there. If we can find Edgar, maybe you could take him to your sister's? I hate to leave him here with all this broken glass."

She nodded and knelt down beside Fleur, stroking the dog's head. Daniel heard the paramedics talking with Kermit outside. He couldn't think of the right words to tell Destiny what he wanted to say.

He swore to himself that he'd have her out of danger by this time tomorrow. And when the criminals were all behind bars . . . then the true test of his own courage would begin.

As Serena rose to answer the knock at the front door, Destiny ran a hand through her hair, wondering if it looked as wild as it felt. Probably. But at least it was clean.

"Stay," she ordered sharply as Fleur raised her head in interest. For once her dog seemed content to remain lounging on the couch—an unheard-of luxury at Serena's house—and wait for the visitor to come to her.

The vet had assured Destiny there was no serious damage to Fleur's leg but that she should keep the dog inactive for the next few days. Destiny did not look forward to Fleur's boredom.

"You ought to have a peephole installed." Daniel's voice in the hall suspended her breathing.

"I'll keep that in mind." Her sister sounded as serene as

her name. But Destiny knew Serena was having much too much fun waiting to see Daniel's reaction to the billowy, low-cut, sea green sweater and tight black leggings she had insisted on lending Destiny after her shower.

"Jake Westing's arrest ought to end the attacks on your sister's life," Daniel continued, "but safety precautions are never a bad idea."

He stopped in the entrance to the family room. Destiny suspected her sister's lips were twisting like the Cheshire cat's, but she couldn't see it because she couldn't take her gaze from Daniel's.

Her good sense remembered his insistence that he couldn't afford to become emotionally involved with her. But all her heart remembered was the way it had felt when he kissed her.

"Now that you're here, Daniel, I'm going out," Serena said, sweeping her purse off the TV. "I promised Sarah and Jesse I'd take them out for pizza and a movie tonight. Sarah's at her friend Elizabeth's, so I'm going to pick her up and head over to Jesse's place."

It took a moment for Destiny to realize she was being abandoned. "Reenie—"

"We'll be at the Spicy Sicilian if you need me, Desty. You can update me on the developments when I get back. Probably after nine or so. Bye, guys."

She fled, leaving Destiny and Daniel in an awkward silence.

Destiny broke it with blinding hospitality. "Have a seat. Can I get you anything? Serena's out of her fruit nectar phase, and I think there's some real juice in her fridge, maybe even some soda. Definitely tea. The water's hot."

"No, thanks."

Daniel sat on the edge of Serena's overstuffed recliner

rather than in the space next to Destiny on the couch. She felt a sting of rejection until she remembered that the rest of the couch was already occupied.

"Kerry tells me Fleur is going to be fine." Daniel leaned past her, close, to scratch Fleur behind the ears.

Destiny nodded, noticing the way his hair brushed over his ear, the hint of stubble along his jaw. "Serena insisted that our wounded hero enjoy the place of honor. Little does she know that Fleur thinks she now owns the couch."

Fleur sighed and settled deeper into the yielding softness.

"And I think Edgar's taken up permanent residence on Sarah's pillow."

"I figured he'd make himself right at home." Daniel smiled, but his mind was elsewhere. "Jake Westing isn't talking."

"I'm not surprised. He's no idiot." Destiny's eyes remained on Daniel. If she closed them, she could still see Jake turning toward her, gun in hand, death in his eyes.

Daniel's grim smile surprised her. "Oh, I wouldn't say that."

She waited. He watched her.

"What?" she finally burst out.

"We obtained a warrant to search Westing's apartment," Daniel told her. "It authorized us to search for evidence related to his assaults on you. We didn't find the rifle he used to shoot out your tire. We didn't find the sweatshirt he wore when he attacked you in the park. He was too smart to keep those items."

He pulled out his notebook, and his smile broadened. "But it turns out he wasn't smart enough to delete his e-mail, including a series of correspondences including phrases like 'taking care of the problem' and 'eliminating loose ends.' Maybe he was saving it for blackmail later on. Whatever the case, we now have an e-mail address for the person who hired him."

"Barris Williams?" Destiny asked, the room wavering for an instant. If she'd accepted Jake's invitation to go for coffee, he would have wrapped up the "loose ends" that very morning . . .

"We don't know for certain," Daniel said, his smile fading. "The address is bismarck@hplink.com. We're working on securing another warrant to require Hope Point Link to release the name of the account holder."

"How long will that take?"

"It won't be any sooner than tomorrow."

Destiny tried to hide her shudder. "Bismarck. Does Williams have ties to North Dakota?"

"I don't know. Wasn't Bismarck the German empire builder?"

"Oh." Destiny's cheeks warmed. "Considering the egos involved, I guess that makes more sense."

"Destiny." His voice compelled her to look at him. "It's all right. We're not waiting until tomorrow."

"For the warrant?"

"We may not need it." There was an unfamiliar glint in his eyes. "None of these messages spells out a murder for hire. Without Westing's testimony, even if we can prove this e-mail account belongs to Williams, all our evidence is circumstantial. It's time to change that."

Destiny recognized his expression. It was the look that lit Fleur's face when she was about to pounce on an unsuspecting Edgar. "How do you plan to do that?"

He grinned. The smile wasn't pleasant, but it was infectious. "I've dropped Mr. Bismarck an e-mail from Jake requesting a meeting to receive payment for a successful hit."

"You told him I was dead?" Her voice squeaked.

"And he's agreed to meet Jake at the gazebo in the park this evening at nine o'clock. I think I ought to surprise him."

"Williams."

"I hope so."

"Who else could it be?"

But he was putting away his notebook and didn't respond.

"Daniel—"

"It will all be over tonight. I promise." His gaze held hers, and she believed him. She believed in him. She trusted him. The knowledge frightened her.

"You need me there. In the park," she said.

He froze, but only for an instant. "I don't think so, Millbrook."

"Listen to me." She leaned across the end table toward him. "If you're at the gazebo, this guy is going to know you've got Jake, that the plan is blown. Barris Williams is not going to panic like some TV villain. He'll claim he was simply out taking an evening stroll. Whereas if *I* meet him in the gazebo and pretend to have joined forces with Jake to blackmail him . . ."

"You're staying right here with your sister."

" . . . you'll have hard evidence to use against him."

He leaned forward, too, his nose inches from hers. "Better yet, I can lock you in the holding tank at the police station."

Destiny ignored him. "I've always wanted to work under-cover. Can I wear a wire?"

"In the holding cell?"

She smiled slowly. "I'm right, and you know it, Parks."

"I'm not putting you in any more danger, and that's that."

"The only way I'm going to be safe is if we put this guy away. Besides, you'll be there to look out for me."

He glared at her. Close up, it was a powerful glare, but she was too mesmerized by the glint of shadows and light in his eyes to notice.

The corners of his mouth turned down, etching lines into his face. Without thinking, she brought her fingers up to smooth them. He hadn't had a chance to shave that morning. The stubble tickled her fingertips.

He grabbed her hand. "You're not going to distract me. He might be armed."

"I'm not trying to distract you." It wasn't her fault his lips looked so sensual when he talked. Besides, he hadn't backed away, and his thumb was rubbing the palm of her hand. "You're the professional. I'm sure you'll work out the safest way to arrange it."

"You enjoy it, don't you? Driving me crazy?"

"Is that what I'm doing?" she murmured. Somehow they'd moved closer together, her lips a short breath from his.

"Yes. Absolutely." He frowned at her. "Only an insane person would even consider it."

She lifted her gaze to his. "Letting me in on the sting?"

"No." His frown deepened. "That makes sense. I don't like it. In fact, I hate it. But it makes sense."

"What then?"

But he was already brushing her lips with his, and she was tasting him, nibbling with her teeth, meeting his tongue with hers.

He was right. It was insane. And she didn't care. Didn't care that the kiss burned with the intensity of her feelings, didn't care that she was losing her heart too fast, didn't care that she was risking a hurt that would make what's-his-name's desertion feel about as significant as breaking a fingernail.

As he pulled her closer, helping her around the end of the table into his lap, heat surged along Destiny's nerves. Her fingertips tingled as she touched his face, his hair, his shoulders. She unbuttoned his shirt. She needed to feel him, his skin next to hers. Needed to breathe in his scent.

She touched the dressings the paramedics had left on his chest and shoulder. They matched the smaller one over his left ear.

"That doesn't happen very often," he said, his voice low. She looked up into blue eyes as unguarded as she'd ever seen them. "But it does happen. I'm a cop."

"I know."

"It isn't easy . . . I . . ." He stopped, at a loss.

"It isn't easy loving a cop?" There, she'd said it. The words shimmered in the air between her and Daniel like an electric charge.

"No," he said, his voice rough with emotion. He touched her face, as though testing whether she was really there. "It's not."

"I'm not all that easy to love myself," she said.

"Oh, yes, you are." And he was kissing her again, and once more warmth enveloped her, this time a warmth that filled her heart.

He kissed her mouth, her forehead, her nose, her jaw. He nibbled her ear so she caught her breath. And then she couldn't catch it at all, as he reached under her sweater, running warm, callused hands over her ribs, up to her breasts.

Her softness astonished him. His fingers found her bra clasp, freeing her to his hands. Her nipples tautened under his touch, his own body responding to her pleasure. She shifted in his lap, and his need for her burned him, shocked him.

She tasted like an autumn evening, sweet, seductive, dangerous. All the more dangerous because he wasn't afraid.

Recklessness pulsed like a drumbeat in his veins. Yet he realized he had no reason to fear. Because it was already too late to save himself. It had been too late before he'd tried to push her away.

He would not let common sense push her away from him this time. He would not let anything take her from him again.

"Daniel?"

"Mm?" He nuzzled her neck, one hand running down her ribs to slip between her thighs. The black leggings offered no obstruction to the warmth of his hand, the pressure of his fingers.

"Yes?" he prompted again, but she couldn't speak, couldn't breathe. She dropped her forehead against his shoulder, caught his skin with her teeth as he touched her.

"Daniel," she managed. "The guest bedroom . . ."

"Oh."

It took a tangle of arms and legs for them to rise from the chair, neither one wanting to release the other. Destiny glanced at Fleur. The dog seemed content to sleep on the couch.

Destiny led him down the hall, into a small bedroom that doubled as a sewing room. Swatches of fabric covered the ironing board. A half-made pair of shorts lay on top of the sewing machine. But the bed, though rumpled from Destiny's earlier nap, was clear.

Daniel lifted her sweater over her head, his breath catching at the soft glow of heat that colored her skin. She pushed his shirt over his shoulders, letting it slide to the floor, and then pressed close to him, her skin against his. He pulled her tighter, feeling the warmth of her through his jeans.

She fumbled with his buttons, the heel of her hand pressing against him, making him moan. He helped her out of her leggings, stepping out of his jeans, easing her down onto the bed.

She held his face with her hands, kissing him, pulling him down with her. Her body stretching out beside his, beneath his, felt like a touch of grace.

She pulled back, her eyes wide. "Daniel, this isn't my house . . . I've never . . . I don't know if Serena has any—"

"I do." He reached for his jeans and found the package. She helped him with it. He hadn't known the simple task of putting on a condom could be so arousing.

"Stop." He pushed her hand away, trying to regain any shred of composure.

"Did I do something wrong?"

"No, no. I just . . ." He realized she was teasing him, her skeptical eyes wide and burning with laughter. And more. He kissed her stomach, flicking his tongue into her belly button. "I just want you so much. I want this to be right."

The laughter left her eyes, leaving the other light behind. "It is right, Daniel. It's you."

He came to her then, because he needed her. Because he loved her. And she opened herself to him, welcomed him, reveling in the pressure as he entered her, letting her heat coalesce around his.

Everything but her presence, her touch, her eyes, faded from his mind. The tension of the past week, the terror and cold of that morning, the fear of loving her receded, but not so far that he didn't know how precious this moment was, how much of himself he needed to give to make it real, make it last.

He couldn't get enough of her. He touched her, tasted her, burned inside of her, imprinting her presence on his skin, in his mind. When he felt her release rippling around him, he lowered his mouth to hers, catching her breath, joining her, joining with her in a consummation that left them both shaken.

When he could move again, he shifted his weight from her, brushed her lips with his. He didn't know what to say to her, but she brought a hand up to touch his face, trace his jaw, and he realized he didn't have to say anything. So he pulled the comforter up over them both and held her.

The sharp ringing of a telephone startled Daniel out of the half-doze he'd fallen into. Destiny shifted, reaching for the phone. It felt natural to run a teasing finger down her ribs, over her hip, down the outside of her thigh.

He liked the laughter in her voice when she said hello. But when she turned to look at him, her hand over the mouth-piece, the laughter had disappeared. "It's for you."

For a terrifying split-second his heart threatened to stop. He fumbled for his watch. Four-thirty. He closed his eyes in relief. He hadn't slept long. He hadn't blown the sting.

He nodded at Destiny and carefully climbed over her legs to retrieve his underwear and jeans. He noticed her eyes were sparkling again and decided it wasn't worth hating himself for being distracted. No human being could resist that much temptation. He bit her bare shoulder, exposed by the comforter.

"Sorry, I can't talk on the telephone nude," he whispered.

She held back her laughter as she passed him the phone. "Parks here."

"Danny? I don't know if I should even be calling you about this. But Fiona's my friend and—"

"Tessa?" he interrupted his ex-wife, feeling as though he'd suddenly been transported to the set of a soap opera. He saw Destiny's eyes as she pulled the comforter higher and reached for her sweater. He forced himself to pay attention to the phone. "Tessa, what are you talking about?"

"I came into the station to talk to you, but you weren't

here. Kermit wouldn't give me the number to reach you when
you didn't answer your beeper, but he dialed it for me. I told
him it was important." Typical Tessa, no apology for interrupting him during an investigation. Not to mention what
else she'd interrupted.

"*Is* it important?" he asked.

She must have caught his impatience. "Maybe not. Fine.
If you don't want to hear it—" She stopped herself. "Sorry,
Danny. I feel like a sneak, but it's not your fault. And I'm
angry as hell, but I don't want to . . . It's just that Philip's
been on this kick about the ShopSmart investors and how he
thinks that if Gage really was murdered, the investors might
be the key—"

"Tessa," he cut her off again, "calm down."

"I'm perfectly calm, Daniel."

"Okay. Then take a minute to organize your thoughts and
tell me what's happening."

He could feel her annoyance over the telephone line, but it
focused her. "Philip's been poring over that list of investors
he copied for you. I noticed Barris Williams's name on it.
With me so far?"

"Yes."

"Well, I remembered that money clip you found, and I
began to wonder why you were so interested in it."

Please, Tessa, don't tell me you mentioned it to him.

"And I looked again at the amount of money he had invested, and it wasn't astronomical, but I began to wonder:
Even on Barris's income, how could he afford a new car and
his time-share and all that, plus invest that kind of money?"

"Did you ask him?"

She didn't answer, and his stomach began to hurt.
"Tessa?"

"No."

He closed his eyes in relief.

"No. I should have. He's a partner in my firm. But I thought I'd poke around a little more. I've spent too much time with detectives." He could hear the self-disgust in her voice. "And when I began to suspect . . . well, I just kept poking. Danny, Barris Williams has been embezzling from the firm."

"Has he?" His voice remained calm. He had a suspicion that his satisfaction at the news would only make her feel worse.

"For a long time. He's been juggling money in and out of the books. Lots of money. The creep." He heard her take a deep breath. "I don't know if this has anything to do with Gage or not, but if it does, I thought you should know. I hope I'm not doing the wrong thing."

"Tessa, even if it had nothing to do with Gage, it would be the right thing. Embezzlement is a crime. You'd want him prosecuted for that, wouldn't you?"

He waited.

"Danny, you drive me nuts, you know that?"

"This could be very important information, Tessa. Thank you. Stay away from Williams for now, okay?"

"Just call me Benedict Arnold." The phone clicked.

He hung it up.

Destiny stood in the bedroom doorway, hugging the loose sweater around her. "I'm reheating the tea water. Do you want some?"

He bent down to retrieve his shirt. "Come over here a minute." He heard her reluctant approach. When she was within arm's length, he reached over to catch her hand.

"Tessa says Barris Williams has been embezzling from their firm."

"Really? That's great news," she said.

203

He pulled her closer, until she sat beside him on the bed. "Destiny—"

"It's nothing. I'm sorry. I didn't mean to be silly—"

"Ask me." That brought her gaze back to his.

"Ask you what?"

"Ask me."

She bit her lip, looked away, looked back. "I can tell you still care about her."

"Tessa? Yes. I do."

"Are you still in love with her?"

Solemnly, he shook his head.

She couldn't resist his puppy-dog look. "Are you sure?"

"I'm sure. Do you want me to tell you just how sure I am?"

In her eyes, he saw that she'd caught the change in his tone. She shook her head, throwing him off.

"Don't." She gripped hard the hand that held hers. "If you still want to, you can tell me tonight, after we've caught Barris Williams."

After the case was closed.

"After we've caught Williams." But he let his eyes say it anyway. What he felt for her. Then he rose, pulling her to her feet. "You still want to wear that wire?"

Chapter 13

Light from the single lamp in front of the gazebo filtered through the fog in a silver haze. Lozenges of pale illumination glowed through the latticework, but Destiny could barely see the fingers she wiggled in front of her eyes.

She shivered and stuffed her hands into her jacket pockets, though the damp air wasn't particularly cold. She felt as if she'd been waiting alone in the dark for hours, though it couldn't have been more than fifteen minutes.

She knew Daniel and Kermit haunted the woods outside, but she still felt terribly alone. She wished Fleur were with her. Or better yet, that she was with Fleur back at Serena's, sharing the couch and a bowl of popcorn.

"How are you doing in there?" Daniel's voice in her ear was a lifeline.

"Fine," she answered, keeping her own voice as low and calm as she could manage. She spoke toward the microphone hidden under her jacket. "What time is it?"

"He should be here any minute."

"Okay." She wanted to say more, to beg him not to stop talking, but she took a deep breath instead and ran an inventory of her pockets to keep her mind busy.

She fingered a square of paper she thought might be a movie ticket stub, a gum wrapper, two dog cookies, a tissue that seemed to have gone through the wash with her jacket at least once, her key chain . . .

"Here he comes." Daniel's tense whisper shot adrenaline to her heart. "Kerry's got a visual of someone on the path. Remember how we rehearsed it. Stay calm. If anything feels wrong, call us in. Got it?"

"I'm ready," she lied, taking her position to the right side of the gazebo entrance. She was supposed to stay between Williams and the exit.

She heard footsteps and breathing, though the man approaching was being careful to skirt the gravel in the center of the path.

"Five yards," Daniel whispered, barely a breath of sound through the receiver in her ear. "I see . . . *it's not Williams.*"

Who? Please, not Pleasance Geary. But she didn't speak. The person approaching had already reached the gazebo steps. Rubber-soled shoes scraped on the cement.

Daniel's voice again, a rough, agonized curse. "Destiny, it's Philip Brooks."

"Philip?" the name popped out of her mouth before she remembered the man at the gazebo entrance could hear her.

A sudden burst of light blinded her, and she stumbled back against an iron bench.

"Destiny Millbrook?" Philip sounded as surprised as she was. "What are you doing here? Oh, sorry."

Instead of swinging the flashlight at her head as she half expected, he pointed it toward the floor so she could see again. He'd hidden his blond hair under a dark blue crocheted winter cap, complete with a fuzzy ball on top. But his green eyes were as serious as a stalking cat's.

Every response she'd practiced with Daniel dried up in her mouth. For a moment all she could do was wish she'd never talked Daniel into letting her come out here. She'd liked these people. Jake Westing. Barris Williams. But especially Philip Brooks with his almost shy charm and his care for his grieving sister.

She wanted to turn tail and run home.

Instead, she met Philip's gaze, cocking her head. "Surprised to see me?"

"In a word? Yes." She saw his forehead furrow in the second before he flicked off the flashlight. The world disappeared into darkness, nothing around her but empty space.

She opened her mouth to scream for Daniel, but Philip didn't move closer. In fact, she heard him stepping away.

"What are you doing here?" he asked again, sharp, tense. But Destiny thought he sounded much too cool for someone who'd just run into a woman who was supposed to be dead. *If anything feels wrong, just call us in.* Well, this felt wrong. All wrong. But if Philip Brooks was behind the hell she'd faced over the past week, if he'd hired Jake Westing to kill his own brother-in-law, she'd be damned if she was going to let him get away with it. She'd wrangle a confession out of him if it killed her.

She immediately wished she hadn't phrased her thoughts quite that way.

"I'm here to see you," she said, visualizing how Kinsey Millhone or V. I. Warshawski would handle this type of situation. She decided they would have brought a gun. Barring that, she tried for attitude. "I'm here to make you an offer you can't refuse."

She could see his outline now against the lamplight-laced lattice wall.

"What kind of offer? Where's Williams?"

"Williams?"

"Yes. Barris Williams. I was supposed to meet him here."

Of course. They were partners. "He hasn't told you yet that I'm supposed to be dead?"

"*What?*" Once again the flashlight exploded in her eyes. "Sorry." He pointed the light at the floor. "Didn't mean to blind you. What are you talking about?"

"Destiny." Daniel's voice in her ear. "You've got more company coming. It looks like Williams. I don't like this. Do you want us to move in?"

"No!"

"What?" Philip's habitual control slipped. He sounded as rattled as she was beginning to feel. "Destiny—"

"Shh!" she hissed. "Someone's coming."

"I don't want you alone in there with both of them," Daniel said as Williams's footsteps approached.

"This isn't good," Philip muttered, flicking the flashlight off and leaving the wall to move closer to her.

"Stay back!"

The command in her harsh whisper worked on both Philip and Daniel. Nothing moved in the fog-shrouded woods except the approaching lawyer. He paused at the gazebo entrance. Destiny knew how it felt to leave the light-touched path and step into the featureless dark of the structure.

She held her breath and guessed Philip must be doing the same.

"Jake?" Williams sounded tense but eager. "Are you there?"

"Jake?" Philip asked, his voice taking on a note of desperation. "What the hell is going on, Barris?"

"Philip!" Williams shifted gears into bright greeting. "You're early."

He stepped into the gazebo. Destiny could see him outlined in the doorway, his hair a spidery halo about his round head.

"I've asked a friend of mine to meet us here. I believe you know him. Jake Westing."

"Jake's my law clerk. What does he have to do with this? I thought you wanted this meeting to be confidential."

"All in good time, my friend," Williams said, as though

speaking to a querulous child. "All will be explained. Jake has been running some important errands for me, and I think his talents may prove useful this evening. Now, as for those accounts you were telling me about? Just a moment, I've got a lantern here. . . ."

"For heaven's sake." Philip's frustration was almost palpable. "Are you going to help me trace these bogus ShopSmart investors, or are you too busy playing spymaster? I thought meeting this way was pretty paranoid, but I was willing to respect your fear of reprisals if Salton Enterprises found out you were helping me."

"Philip, Philip . . ." A match flickered as Williams hunkered over his propane lantern.

"But now I find out you've got my own employee working as your errand boy. People offering me deals 'I can't refuse.' What I refuse is to be cast in your B-grade gangster movie.

"And as for you—" Philip turned to face Destiny, a darker shadow in the dark. "—before I go, I want to know how you're mixed up in this farce, Destiny."

A hiss, propane and human, sputtered through the gazebo, and suddenly the lantern illuminated them all, eyes wide, like three animals caught in an eighteen-wheeler's headlights.

In that instant Destiny knew how it felt to see a ghost, because she could see the shock and horror of it in Barris Williams's face. His eyes rounded in a parody of surprise, his mouth worked, but no sound emerged.

She glanced at Philip, who was staring at Williams in puzzled frustration. She wanted to hug him, to apologize for thinking he could be a killer.

"You—You're dead!" Williams choked out. His eyes looked like O's.

Destiny smiled. "Disappointed?"

"Jake!" Williams shouted, jumping to his feet. He looked around wildly. "Jake! Where are you?"

"What the—" Philip started forward, but Destiny stopped him with a gesture.

"Jake's not coming tonight," she said, her voice calm despite the anger that shook through her.

"He said you were dead," Williams said, almost plaintively, staring at her.

"He lied." She clenched her fists in her pockets. "Jake and I made a little deal, Mr. Williams. He wasn't satisfied with his last paycheck."

"That slimy little—" Williams's face reddened, the cords in his neck distended. "I'll kill him! I paid him good money to take care of you! He kept screwing it up, and I still paid him more! The greedy, unprincipled . . ." His voice dissolved in rage.

Daniel's voice hissed in Destiny's ear. "That's enough. I've got it on tape. We're moving in."

"Wait!" Destiny stepped forward, closer to Williams, her fury for the moment overpowering his. "I don't care how much you paid Jake, Mr. Williams. You're going to have to start paying me now. And not just for attempted murder. Philip and I are going to demand a hefty reward to keep quiet about your part in Gage Barclay's death."

"You? You *murdered* Gage?" Philip gasped.

Destiny had hoped to trap Williams into a further confession, but she'd forgotten Philip wasn't aware of the plan. Philip's fine-boned face twisted into a mask of rage, and he lunged toward Williams's throat.

For a small, middle-aged man, Williams moved with surprising speed and strength. He dodged Philip's attack, kicking out with a heavy foot that caught the younger man's shin and sent him crashing into one of the iron benches.

Before Destiny could move forward to assist Philip, she saw the flash of silver in Barris Williams's hand. His palm overwhelmed the little gun, which looked more like a toy than a weapon. In the golden circle of lamplight, the scene looked so surreal that Destiny hardly felt her fear.

"You're not going to get away with this!" Williams shouted, the arm with the gun waving in his agitation. "I worked all my life just to get where I am, and you're not going to destroy it. Not you—" He pointed the gun at Philip, then Destiny. "—and not you. And not that sniveling, snot-nosed Westing. I'll kill you all."

"Police! Drop the gun!"

Destiny whirled toward the sound of Daniel's voice, relief washing over her. She'd almost forgotten the police were there.

But in that moment of letting down her guard, Williams reached her, yanking her back by her hair and jamming his gun under her chin.

"Stay back!" His voice burst harsh and shrill against Destiny's ear. "Stay back or I'll kill her! I swear I will!"

Daniel felt his heart stop. His body went cold. He no longer felt blood pulsing in his veins. From his new position to the right of the gazebo entrance, he could see Barris Williams, the man's face twisted in rage and fear. And Destiny.

"Should I see if I can get a clean shot?"

Kermit's low voice beside him snapped him out of his paralysis. *Focus. Don't think about failure.*

"If we shoot him now, she's dead. Get him in your sights, but wait for my signal." He pulled off his headset and microphone and pushed them at Kermit. "Talk to her. Keep her calm. Tell her we're going to get her out of this."

Kermit nodded and eased away around the azalea bushes.

Daniel rose from his crouch, his gun raised, and stepped into the light that brushed the gazebo entrance. Three slow, careful steps and he stood on the gazebo floor, outlined in the arched entryway.

He could see Destiny's eyes now, see the fear. And he could see the apology for letting herself be taken hostage. He held her with his gaze, tried to tell her he wouldn't let her be hurt. Not exactly the easiest message to convey considering that he was sighting down the barrel of his .38, aiming inches from her forehead.

"Put down the gun, Williams," Daniel said, his voice cool despite his pounding heart. "We've got you surrounded. Don't make things worse for yourself."

"Don't come a step closer," Williams warned. "You're going to back away and let me out of here, or I'll kill her. You don't want to see this young lady's brains sprayed all over the wall."

Daniel seriously doubted that Williams's little .22 would spray anyone's brains anywhere, but that wouldn't make much difference to Destiny if Williams pulled the trigger. In his head, he could hear the shot already, but his aim never wavered.

"Brooks, are you all right?"

Philip shifted from his position crumpled against a bench. "I'm not sure."

"I want you out of here."

"I can't walk yet."

He heard the pain in Philip's voice, but he never took his eyes off Williams.

"Both of you leave," Williams demanded. "Back out."

Daniel shook his head. "I can't do that."

Williams's eyes widened, and he tilted Destiny's head back to show the gun pressed into her flesh. "You can, and you will."

Caught between the desire to blow a hole through Williams's left eye socket and the temptation of conceding to the man's demands, Daniel felt his training kick in.

"Let her go, Williams." *Keep him focused on you, on your words.* "You don't want to do this. It's over." Soothing. Logical. Convince him it's his only choice. "Jake was the violent one, not you. Drop the gun and let her go."

He could see the wavering in the lawyer's eyes as Williams began to realize that he wasn't going to walk out of the gazebo a free man. This was a dangerous moment if Williams panicked.

"That's right," Daniel said, as though agreeing with Williams's inner thoughts. "This isn't worth it."

"It's all Jake's fault," Williams burst out, his face crumpling. "I never wanted to kill anyone. I hired Jake to convince Gage Barclay to vote for the ShopSmart project. If he couldn't see what was best for his constituents, Jake was supposed to keep him away from the voting meeting. That's all. I only wanted Gage to listen to reason."

"He wouldn't back down."

"The ShopSmart development will benefit the whole community. But would Gage see that? No. He was a radical. Hurting everyone just to preserve some bloody pastureland. Now cows have more rights than people do?"

"You were frustrated," Daniel sympathized, watching for any shifting of Williams's gun. "But you didn't mean to hurt anybody."

"Can you imagine how I felt when Gage died?" Williams asked, his gaze meeting Daniel's, begging for understanding. "How was I to know Jake Westing was a psychopath? After the plane crash, he came to me, threatened to expose me if I didn't pay him the money. What could I do? It would have ended there if Miss Millbrook hadn't been in the park that night."

Daniel saw Destiny's eyes narrow. He broke in before she could refocus Williams's anger on herself. "Getting rid of her was Westing's idea, wasn't it? He's the one who followed her and tried to strangle her."

Williams nodded, eyes wide with tortured innocence. Daniel wanted to break his nose. Instead, he tsked sympathetically.

"You know what Westing's going to say if you hurt Ms. Millbrook, don't you?" he asked. "Do you want to give his defense team that kind of ammunition? Give yourself up. Give your own lawyers a chance."

For the first time, Williams eased his gun from Destiny's throat. Not far, but it was progress. Daniel reminded himself to breathe.

"That's right. Toss the gun to the floor, and let her go. No one has to get hurt."

"I never wanted to hurt anyone," Williams parroted, almost as though he believed it himself. "I just wanted what I deserved. I worked hard to get where I am. I didn't have everything handed to me on a silver platter like the Gage Barclays of the world.

"If this development project went through, I could have repaid all the money I borrowed from the firm. No one would ever have known. No one hurt. I deserved it!"

Grimacing with tension, Williams inched his pistol from Destiny's neck, turning it out and away.

"Good," Daniel encouraged him. "Now toss it aside."

Williams met his gaze again, an almost petulant expression in his eyes. "I deserved it."

In that moment, with Daniel's and Williams's attention focused tautly on each other, Philip Brooks struck. He launched himself from his crouch like a panther striking.

"I'll show you what you deserve!"

Williams's gun jerked. Destiny screamed. Philip's body blocked Daniel's shot. Philip plowed into Williams and Destiny with nearly equal force.

A gunshot ricocheted off the concrete floor with a wicked ping, immediately followed by a crack like a hundred firecrackers. The propane cylinder of the lantern exploded into shrapnel. And fire fell on the wooden latticework of the gazebo like rain.

Destiny hit the concrete floor with a thud that knocked the air from her body, though her head was protected by Barris Williams's rib cage.

The explosion of light blinded her. The blast deafened her. Her fear and the fire dancing in the sudden blackness were too far away to matter.

Williams jerked beneath her, sending her head cracking to the floor. She couldn't hear her own complaint. She knew she had to crawl away from him, but her limbs wouldn't cooperate. She struggled out from under a heavy weight on her legs. Philip.

She touched his shoulder. He shifted, his lips moving. Her hand came away sticky and red.

Still dazed, she looked up, her gaze caught by the intricate patterns of the flames as they licked up the walls and began weaving through the lattice ceiling.

"Destiny!"

She wasn't sure she heard Daniel's voice as much as felt it. But when she turned, he was there, his hands grabbing her arms, pulling her into an embrace she couldn't have escaped if she wanted to. She didn't want to.

He said something she couldn't hear. She shook her head as he released her, and she pointed down.

"Philip!" she shouted, trying to overpower the flames and

her own deafness. "He's hurt!"

She tried to read Daniel's words. He pointed to the fire. " . . . got to get him out of here!"

He bent down and pulled Philip's arm over his shoulder. Destiny grabbed the man's other arm and heaved, helping Daniel lift him to his feet. Philip's eyes didn't focus, but he struggled to get his feet planted.

They turned to the gazebo entrance. Flames leaped from one side of the archway to the other. She looked at Daniel. He mouthed the words, "Drop and roll." She nodded.

As they gathered their strength, he paused and turned. Shouts penetrated the haze in her head. It sounded like Kermit's voice, right inside her ear. The microphone receiver.

Daniel touched her shoulder and pointed. They turned Philip, facing the other side of the gazebo.

A ragged hole in the lattice wall showed the dark azalea bushes outside. Destiny saw Kermit swinging a heavy tree limb, breaking away the flimsy wall, shouting at them to hurry.

Daniel and Destiny supported Philip, stumbling, to the new exit. Dropping his branch, Kermit reached in and pulled Philip through the hole, dragging him through the azaleas.

"Go!" Daniel shouted in Destiny's ear. She could hear him now. "Follow Kermit. I'll get Williams."

But he didn't have to. A hand grabbed the collar of Destiny's jacket and turned her toward Daniel, Williams using her as a shield between himself and Daniel as he moved toward escape.

Smoke burned Destiny's lungs; bruises throbbed along her hips and shoulders and the back of her head; her throat still ached from Williams's gun. She thought about Gage Barclay dead, Jake Westing in jail, Philip injured.

"I've had just about enough of this!" she shouted, stuffing her hand into her jacket pocket. She pulled out a fistful of keys. Spinning around, she jabbed her fist hard into Williams's throat.

She missed his windpipe. But the sudden surprise and pain loosened his hold on her jacket. She pulled free, blocking the hole in the lattice wall with her body.

Roaring with pain and fury, Williams whirled away from her, toward the fire-engulfed entrance. Daniel reached him in two lunging strides.

Together they plunged through the flames.

Chapter 14

"Daniel!" The scream tore from Destiny's throat.

"Destiny, get out of there. This way." Kermit's voice sounded in her ear, jolting her back from panic.

She turned and bolted through the open hole, a cool haven of darkness in the spreading flames. Kermit helped her jump to the ground three feet below.

"Daniel and Williams," she gasped. "They went out the front."

Kermit nodded and led the way through the azaleas. They burst onto the path that ringed the gazebo. Destiny saw Philip huddled against the trunk of a redwood tree.

She ran on, her feet crunching the gravel, Kermit's long legs outdistancing her as they turned the corner toward the gazebo entrance. She could see movement, black shapes writhing in the red light, the night dancing to the rhythm of fire.

Frantically, her eyes picked two solid shapes out of the shadows licking the pale gravel. Kermit reached them first, yanking a pair of handcuffs free of his belt. One of the shapes shifted aside, then rose, disentangling himself from the night. She recognized his rugged profile as he turned to look for her.

"Daniel." She had no strength left to shout, but he heard her. Strong hands grabbed her shoulders, touched her face. She grabbed him back, reassured by his solidity and the strong beat of his pulse beneath her hands.

She couldn't see any burns on him, though a patch of his hair looked darker than the rest. When she touched it, it brushed away to nothing beneath her fingers.

"Are you hurt?" he asked, the words strained by emotion.

"Cuts and bruises. You?"

"The same." Still he held her a little away from him, his eyes drinking her in. "I knew this was a bad idea."

Destiny tried to ignore the frisson of doubt that shivered through her. "We caught him, didn't we?"

"Yes."

"It's over." She tried not to plead. If he'd changed his mind . . .

"Thank God," he said. "I've never been so terrified in my life."

"*I* was the one with the gun stuck in my throat," she reminded him.

He brushed her cheek with his thumb. "You were wonderful."

"No." She shook her head. "I knew you wouldn't let him shoot me."

His face darkened. She saw the reflection of fear in his eyes. "Destiny—"

"I was right, wasn't I?" She tried a smile. "At least this time."

"Destiny, there isn't going to be a next time."

A chill touched her heart. He'd warned her. Warned her he wouldn't allow himself to be involved with anyone who might compromise his professionalism. But she hadn't listened. She'd thought the feelings they shared would be enough to change his mind, change his heart.

"Daniel . . ." Her pride stuck in her throat, but she continued. "Don't decide this right now. Please. Think—"

"No. This is it." He frowned down at her. She looked for doubt in his eyes, but there was none. "You are not entering the park after sunset again."

She stared at him.

"Don't look at me like that. I don't care if it's sexist and overprotective. You've almost been killed here two times in the last ten days. I don't think it's too much to ask. I might not survive another night like tonight."

She knew she'd sound nuts if she laughed, but she couldn't help it. "But it's so lovely and peaceful out here at night."

"It's lovely and peaceful in my living room at night," Daniel said, "and I can build a nice, blazing fire without shrapnel. And for a limited time, I can even throw in a fresh evening breeze through my paneless window frames."

She stepped toward him then, and he pulled her close, lowering his mouth to meet hers with all the fierceness of his fear. Destiny wanted never to leave his arms, never to break the kiss, even when sirens pierced the night and the shouts of policemen echoed through the trees.

Daniel kissed her nose, as reluctant as she to break away. "That was fast."

"Kermit called for backup and an ambulance while you were convincing Williams not to shoot me." She tapped her ear. "I heard him using his radio."

Daniel's brow furrowed. "Can you hear him now?"

"Sure."

She thought again what an effective scowl Daniel could muster as he tugged open the zipper of her jacket to reveal the microphone.

"Kerry!" he bellowed. She heard a yelp of pain in her ear. "Turn this blasted thing off!"

The fluorescent lighting and late hour imbued Daniel's office with an unreality that even the sludgy departmental coffee couldn't dispel. Destiny looked into the murky depths of her cup. After all that the Hope Point Police Department had done for her recently, maybe she ought to buy them a decent coffee machine to show her appreciation. She could very well be saving lives that way.

A hand on her shoulder brought her out of her contemplation with a start.

"Sorry, I didn't mean to surprise you." Daniel held a chipped and stained coffeepot in his hand. "I thought you might want a refill."

"You did?" She couldn't hide her disbelief.

He laughed and set the pot down on his desk. "Okay, maybe I just wanted to see that look on your face. How are you? You ready to go home?"

Home . . . Fleur . . . a soft bed. The prospect was dazzling. Yet she was reluctant to break the spell of safety she felt here in Daniel's office. He looked relaxed, competent, leaning a hip against his desk, his sandy brown hair as rumpled as his shirt. She moved to lean beside him.

"That's it?" she asked. "Have you heard from the hospital? How's Philip?"

"Lucky." Daniel shook his head. "The idiot. He got a couple cracked ribs from falling against that bench and some nasty lacerations from the propane lantern exploding. Nothing a little rest and some stitches won't mend."

"What was he doing there in the first place? When he showed up, I thought . . ."

"Me, too." He squeezed her shoulder. "He was so adamant that Gage wasn't murdered. And he was involved in the ShopSmart project. When I found out Jake Westing worked for him, I was afraid he might be mixed up in Gage's death."

Daniel ran a hand through his hair. "Actually, he was involved, in a way. In two ways, really. Philip was the one who mentioned to Barris Williams you were dating a cop."

Destiny flushed. "It was that day in the library. I tried to tell him I wasn't."

"Williams had already seen us together in the park and recognized me from my connection with Tessa. He thought he recognized you, too, from the library, and when he saw you at the reference desk with the scarf to cover your bruises, he knew you had to be the one who had overheard him and Jake that Friday night. Once he and Jake realized you weren't coming home after Jake's sniper attack on your car, it didn't take him long to figure out you might be with me."

"You said Philip was involved in two ways."

"Philip had been looking into the backgrounds of the major investors in the development project. He found phony names on the list. Since he knew Barris Williams was working on the project, Philip thought Williams might be able to explain the discrepancy. Of course, it never occurred to him that those phony names were fronts for Williams himself, who'd used them to invest money embezzled from his own law firm.

"Williams told Philip he knew something shady was going on, but he was afraid of repercussions if anyone at Salton Enterprises found out he was helping Philip investigate."

"So they had to meet at an isolated spot, with no witnesses . . ." Destiny shuddered.

"Where Williams thought he would first meet Jake Westing to pay him for successfully taking you out of the picture. I guess Williams figured Jake wouldn't balk at killing his boss."

"I'm sure he was right. I just can't understand why Jake, why anyone, would be willing to kill . . ."

Daniel took her hand and squeezed it. She realized it wasn't Daniel's office that created her sense of safety there. It was Daniel's solid presence that kept the terror of the past several hours at bay.

"If Williams was willing to kill Philip, who knows where he would have stopped." Her voice felt funny, shaky. "Maybe it was easier after the first one, after he had Jake murder Gage Barclay . . ."

"But he didn't."

"Didn't what?"

"Contract to have Gage Barclay murdered."

She leaned away from the desk to look up at him. "What are you talking about?"

"Have I told you how incredibly sexy it is when you look at me like I'm out of my mind?"

"No." She'd file it away for future reference. But she was too sensible to be distracted by a mere compliment, however much her toes tingled. "You think Williams did it himself and then blamed it on Jake? He *is* a lying snake."

"Funny, that's exactly what Westing said."

"Jake talked to you?"

Daniel's smile was slow and predatory. "I played a little bit of the tape I recorded this evening for our friend Jake. Hearing Williams rat on him encouraged him to talk."

"I can imagine." She let Daniel pull her closer once more. She gulped her coffee, hoping to settle the fluttering in her stomach. Big mistake. She set the cup down with a grimace.

"Jake's description of their agreement ought to help put Williams away for a very long time. But Jake also corroborated Williams's account of his original plan. Jake's job was to do whatever it took—threats, embarrassment, bribes, sabotage—to convince Gage Barclay to vote in favor of the ShopSmart development."

"And Jake took it too far."

"No." Daniel's expression twisted. "The FAA didn't miss

any evidence in the plane crash. Gage's death was an accident. Just an accident. You can imagine Jake's disappointment when Gage died. He knew Williams wouldn't pay for an accident, so he took credit for it."

Destiny studied Daniel's face. "I can't believe it." She almost didn't want to believe it. "But . . . that sounds exactly like Jake."

"Yeah." Daniel's blue eyes were dark and grim. "Even if you'd overheard their entire conversation that night in the park and turned them in, the most they could have been convicted of was conspiring to influence a public official. Now they're looking at conspiracy to commit murder, assault with a deadly weapon, resisting arrest, shooting a police officer—I'm making a list."

"Embezzlement, fraud, breaking and entering," Destiny added.

"Wait, wait." Daniel patted his jacket. "Let me find a pencil."

It felt good to laugh. "Here, let me." Destiny wiggled her hands under his jacket, running her fingers over his ribs.

"Aaah!" He jerked back.

"What?"

"That tickles!"

"What? That?"

"Aaah! Stop!"

She did, her hands sliding around his back, as he pulled her around in front of him. She met his gaze. "And Pleasance Geary wasn't involved?"

"Not in any way."

"Then it's really over?"

"You mean other than the paperwork and the grand jury indictment and testifying at the trial and—aaah! Yes. It's over."

"Case closed?"

His eyes darkened, and she could feel the awkward thumping of her heart. He lifted a hand to touch her cheek. "Case closed."

"Does that mean—" Her throat closed, and she tried again. "Does that mean I won't be a distraction anymore?"

"Destiny . . ." He brushed a thumb across her lips, sending liquid electricity through her. "I'd have to be dead for you not to distract me."

He bent toward her, then stopped, his lips inches from hers, to look into her eyes. "Oh. You mean from my job?"

She would have smacked him, but the warmth in his eyes melted her muscles.

"I've learned a lot of things this week," he said, his voice serious. "And one of them is that I can be both a police officer *and* a human being. Not that it's easy to balance the two. But I can do it. Because I also learned that neither one of those things means much to me if I can't be with you."

His eyebrows rumpled. "I know it's too soon, too sudden."

Destiny wondered if she'd float up off the floor if he released her. "Daniel—"

"Shh." He pressed a finger to her lips. "Don't interrupt. I'm trying to tell you I love you here."

She wrapped her fingers around his and pulled his hand away. She could feel his pulse beating with hers.

"You're right. It's too soon, too sudden. But as you said to me a long time ago—this morning?—that doesn't mean it's not happening." For one second she thought of Alain, remembered what it felt like to risk love and lose. But she loved Daniel far too much to deny what she felt. And Daniel wasn't going to desert her. As Serena had pointed out . . .

"Oh, shoot."

"What?" He paused, his lips inches from hers.

"Not you," she assured him. "Serena. She'll never let me hear the end of it."

"Of what?"

She peeped up at him. "You remember I told you I went into the park that Friday night to commune with the full moon? Because Serena said it would be good for me?"

She gave him credit for hiding his smile. "I remember. Your life was in a rut."

"I didn't tell you the whole story. Serena told me that if I went out and basked in the moonlight, I'd . . . I'd meet a man. My soul mate."

He raised his eyebrows.

"And find true love."

"And?"

"And what?"

"Was she right?"

She saw his concern and his own doubt, his courage in the face of fear. She saw it, and she knew he loved her. She knew . . .

"I love you, Daniel Parks. I love you more than I thought was possible."

"I can't tell you how good it feels to hear you say that," he murmured, brushing her hair back from her face, the tips of his fingers trailing against her cheek. He saw her frown. "What's wrong?"

"Aren't you going to kiss me now?"

"Oh."

And he did.

DATE DUE			
		HFRAW	PENDE
PENDERGRASS, TESS			
DANGEROUS MOONLIGHT			

HFRAW   PENDE